Gina McMurchy-Barber

Free as a bird

DUNDURN PRESS
TORONTO

Edited by Michael Carroll
Designed by Courtney Horner
Printed and bound in Canada by Webcom

Library and Archives Canada Cataloguing in Publication

McMurchy-Barber, Gina
    Free as a bird / Gina McMurchy-Barber.

ISBN 978-1-55488-447-6

I. Title.

PS8625.M86F74 2009   jC813'.6   C2009-903256-2

1 2 3 4 5   14 13 12 11 10

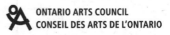

Canada

Conseil des Arts du Canada / Canada Council for the Arts

ONTARIO ARTS COUNCIL
CONSEIL DES ARTS DE L'ONTARIO

We acknowledge the support of the **Canada Council for the Arts** and the **Ontario Arts Council** for our publishing program. We also acknowledge the financial support of the **Government of Canada** through the **Book Publishing Industry Development Program** and **The Association for the Export of Canadian Books**, and the **Government of Ontario** through the **Ontario Book Publishers Tax Credit program**, and the **Ontario Media Development Corporation**.

Care has been taken to trace the ownership of copyright material used in this book. The author and the publisher welcome any information enabling them to rectify any references or credits in subsequent editions.

J. Kirk Howard, President

www.dundurn.com

Dundurn Press	Gazelle Book Services Limited	Dundurn Press
3 Church Street, Suite 500	White Cross Mills	2250 Military Road
Toronto, Ontario, Canada	High Town, Lancaster, England	Tonawanda, NY
M5E 1M2	LA1 4XS	U.S.A. 14150

Mixed Sources
Product group from well-managed forests, controlled sources and recycled wood or fiber
www.fsc.org Cert no. SW-COC-002358
© 1996 Forest Stewardship Council
FSC

ANCIENT FOREST ™
FRIENDLY

For my parents,
Gene and Murray McMurchy,
whose dedication to my sister, Jane, taught me everything
I need to know about unconditional love

acknowledgements

I would like to thank my generous friend, Victoria Bartlett, for her time and wise guidance; Jane Cassie and Karen Autio for their helpful comments; the Surrey Public Library's Writer-in-Residence Program and Mansel Robinson for his gentle feedback and insights; and my friend, Kathy, for setting me straight on a few facts.

Ombudsman Dulcie McCallum's report, *The Need to Know: Administrative Review of Woodlands School*, and Michael de Courcy's photographic exhibition/archive entitled *Asylum: A Long Last Look at Woodlands*, were very helpful to me in re-creating the atmosphere and attitudes of the time.

I would also like to acknowledge and thank those former residents of Woodlands who have spoken out about their experiences — giving me and others a better understanding of what they had to endure.

chapter 1

My name's Ruby Jean Sharp an I growed up in Woodlands School. That wasn't a nice place for a liddle kid — nope, not a nice place a'tall. Sometimes the uniforms was happy with me — that's how come they called me Sharp-as-a-Tack. But there was other times when they wasn't happy — that's cause I'd scratch or bite or wet my pants. Uniforms said I did that cause I was a bad kid … said I had a behaviour problem. Maybe they was right. But maybe I jus dint like bein bossed round all the time or sittin all day with nothin to do cept go stir crazy. Maybe it was cause I dint like standin naked in the tub room an gettin sprayed down with cold water. Whatever it was made me behave bad — them uniforms had ways to make me stop. Sometimes they hit me or shouted an called me names like retard. They called me that on account of me not bein so smart.

I dint always scratch an bite an pee my pants — nope, not a'tall. It started after Mom an Harold left me at Woodlands School when I was eight years old. Can't say why they called it a school — a school's a place you go for learnin an then after you get to go home. I never learnt much bout ledders and numbers, an I sure never got to go home — nope, only stayed at Woodlands all day an all night. I lived on Ward 33.

Mom said cause I wasn't so smart I dint knowed too many things. Maybe she was right, but I sure membered the day she left me at Woodlands — yup, I membered everythin bout it. First thing that mornin Mom said to put on my good dress — the one Gramma gave me with the white polka dots. After a long drive we went through a big gate an parked the car. Walkin up the path I held Mom's hand, an Barbra too — Barbra was my best doll. Harold walked hind us — quiet as a mouse. Harold was my mom's boyfriend. I guess Mom an Harold was mad at me that day, cause they dint talk or smile or even look at me.

We came to a big yellow buildin but the door was locked — yup, locked tight. Then a man in white opened the door an we followed him upstairs. I liked hearin our footsteps boomin all the way to the top so I stomped my feet hard to make it louder. Mom squeezed my hand an said, "Stop it, Ruby Jean. Just stop it."

When we got to the top floor there was another locked meddal door. I thought it sure was a awful good thing the man in white had so many keys so's we could get in all them locked doors. When we walked down the hall there was lotsa kids. Only they dint look like real kids — I think maybe cause they wasn't happy. I said hello to some of em, but no one said hello back. Some kids drooled an made moanin noises when we walked by. Others crowded round, touchin my hair an Mom's shoulder. Harold got mad when one of the big ones tried to hug him.

I asked Mom why the kids dint look happy, but she squeezed my hand an said, "Stop it, Ruby Jean. Just stop it."

Then we came to nother big door that was locked. It had a liddle window high up — only the big people could see through it. The man in white took out his keys again an unlocked that big green door. That was when I looked inside an saw lots of brown meddal beds. There was a window too — it had thick meddal bars, but was too high for me to look outta. I thought this mus be a place for bad people, an it was a awful good thing they had locks on all the doors — yup, awful good thing.

"So, Ruby Jean," the man said to me. "Welcome to your new home. This is where you're going to sleep." At first I dint understand — I guess on account of me not bein so smart. So I jus stared at him — yup, jus stared. He looked at Mom. "Didn't you talk to her about this?"

I waited for her to tell that man in white he made a mistake, but she dint. "Mrs. Sharp, you were supposed to explain to Ruby Jean what was going to happen today." The man shook his head.

"Ruby Jean — like the man said — this is going to be your new home. Me and Harold are putting you here for your own good. Even Dr. Stone said it was better for you. These people here can teach you things — they have a lot of experience knowing how to deal with kids like you."

Kids like me? She was talkin bout kids who dint think so good or behave how they was spose to. I suddenly membered the sad kids in the hallway an all the locked doors. Can't say how it happened, but my heart started thumpin real hard and jumped right up into my throat — yup, I could feel it poundin away inside there. I dropped Barbra on the floor an pulled my mom's hands an said, "I wanna go now. I wanna go home."

"Now, Ruby Jean, don't you make trouble for me. You got yourself into this mess because you don't listen," Mom's face was turnin red. "You never obeyed anyone except Gramma — that's why she always looked after you — but now she's gone. I know it's not all your fault — you were born this way. But all the same, me and Harold don't want … what I mean to say is we can't handle your misbehaving."

I pulled harder on her hands an said, "No, Mommy, I'll be good, an I promise I will get smarter, I will, I will."

Then she squeezed my hands hard one last time an said, "Stop it, Ruby Jean. Just stop it." That's when the man in white pulled me into the room.

"I'm not bad like these kids, Mommy. I'm a happy girl — a happy, good girl. See, see ... see me smile?" I tried to smile my best smile but Mom an Harold couldn't see cause they was lookin down on the floor. I tried pullin away from the uniform man but he was very strong — yup, too strong for me. When I looked back Mom an Harold was gone. I heard the scuffle of their shoes as they hurried down the hall. I cried after em, "I'll be good, please don't leave me here ... Mom? Harold? Please don't leave me here."

It was on account of me not bein so smart that they left me in this place with locked meddal doors, windows with bars an so many sad kids. The man in the white uniform tried his best to talk to me, but I guess I was jus too scared to listen.

"It'll be all right, Ruby Jean. You'll get use to it. Now come and see your room. Try out your bed and feel how comfy it is. Then I'll take you down to the day room to meet the others." The others? He was talkin bout more kids like those sad, droolin, moanin ones I saw out in the hall.

I picked up Barbra an held her tight an screamed at him, "No, I don't wanna sit on the bed. I wanna go home." I started screamin so loud I musta scared him cause he left me in the room all by myself — yup, closed the door an locked it. Me an Barbra was alone in there cryin for a long time.

That was a sad day an when I think bout it I get sad all over again. Fore then I could only member one other time I was so sad. It was the day Gramma went to heaven in the amblance. That mornin she told me, "Ruby Jean, I'm not feeling myself today." Then a liddle while later the amblance came to the door an took her — yup, an never brought her back.

After Mom an Harold left me at Woodlands I had a lotta sad days — an a lotta things to get use to ... cept I never really got use to em. For one thing I had to share my room with seven other kids an every night one of em was mad or sad bout somethin. The rest of us dint get to sleep till all the ruckus an cryin was done. Nother thing I dint like was the stuff we had to eat. My Gramma was a awful good cook, that's how come I knowed how things was sposed to taste. Fore comin to Woodlands my favourite dessert was Gramma's pudding. But priddy soon I dint like puddin no more on account of it wouldn't stay on my spoon — nope, it was like brown soup. Sides the drippy puddin, the vegables was mushy an the meat was like old gum that lost its chew. An we dint never get to have lemon pie with a dollop of whip cream or pizza with mozza or fish 'n chips wrapped in newspaper — nope, dint getta eat things like that no more.

Worse than all that was how I dint have no say over my own body no more. Had to stand naked in front of the others, had to sit on a toilet with em uniforms watchin, an if I dint go they poured hot water on my privates to make me go — that hurt ... a lot. Nother thing I dint like ... I never gotta say bout what I wanted to wear.

One night, soon after Mom an Harold left me, I woke up in the dark an there was a night uniform layin side me an he was touchin me. I dint like that man touchin me like that — nope, not a'tall. So I scratched an bit him hard's I could. He slapped my face, but that dint stop me from tryin to bite him more.

I membered Gramma tellin me I should get a police man if I ever needed help. So's I told that uniform I was gunna tell the police man bout him. He jus smiled an said, "Is that right?" After that he put me in a skinny room — had only a tiny window an a real cold floor. I tried to kick an scream an stop that uniform from puttin me there but he said I was misbehavin an had to be punished. I stayed there all night — yup, all by myself, shiverin an cryin. I sure dint never wanna be put in that place again, so I decided I was never gunna tell the police man bout that uniform touchin me.

I started bitin a lotta people after that. An when a new uniform came to Ward 33 the others said, "Watch out for that one. She's a biter."

I thought bout runnin away but all em locked doors an barred windows woulda stopped me. An when the uniforms took me outdoors they held on to me tight — yup, awful tight. Well, cept for one day.

It was not so long after I came to Woodlands an I was outside walkin in a line with some other kids. Nurse stopped to talk to somebody. She shook her finger at us kids an said, "You just stand there and wait!" We all stood an waited. But after a while I think Nurse forgot bout us. That's when I started lookin round an saw the road Mom an Harold drove on when they brought me to Woodlands. I thought to myself, if that road brought me in here it mus be able to take me back out. At first I walked way slowly, but then I started to run — faster an faster. I had a feelin I was gunna get away. Yup, I thought — yer gunna get oudda here, Ruby Jean. But then I said to myself — well, where ya gunna go? Mom and Harold's? Do you know how to find them? Would they let ya stay? Suddenly I got smashed down to the ground by a big green uniform. He was on top of me an my face hurt a lot from bein pushed into the rocks an dirt. Then Nurse caught up an yelled at me an told me no more walks for a long time.

After that the uniforms called me a biter an a runner. And whenever I went outside I had to wear a belt-leash round my tummy or sometimes round my wrist. I dint like havin the leash round my wrist cause it made my arm sore — yup, awful sore. Never got nother idea to run away after that — that's cause I dint have no place to go.

It was a long time ago I was eight. I dunno zackly how old I am now on account of me not bein so smart. And sides that — I dint get birthday cakes no more. Fore I came to Woodlands I could always tell how old I was by countin candles on my birthday cakes. All the same, I knowed I was growin cause whenever I saw myself in the mirror I could tell I was gettin taller an rounder in the middle. Nurse said I was plump. I had dark brown hair an small liddle eyes an lotsa freckles too, jus like Gramma. Nother thing that was jus like Gramma's was my smile — everybody use to say so. An even when I dint feel much like it, I smiled at myself in the mirror jus so's I could member what it was like havin her look at me an say, "I love you, Ruby Jean."

Maybe I dint knowed zackly how old I was, but I did know the day I was born. Yup, Gramma use to say over an over, "You came into this world on February 19, 1957, at St. Paul's Hospital in Vancouver. And it was one of the happiest days of my life."

Wasn't one of Mom's happiest days — nope, not a'tall. That's cause after I took so long gettin born the doctor told her I was a retard. He said somethin bout me havin a extra chromosome. Dunno what a chromosome is, but I sure wished I dint have a extra one cause then maybe Mom wouldn't have left me at Woodlands.

Gramma was different — yup, she loved me right from the start. Even if I was … like the doctor said … a retard. She was the one who named me Ruby Jean when I was a baby.

17

"I called you Ruby because you're like a precious jewel and gave you the name Jean because it means 'a gift from the good Lord.' And that's just what you are, Ruby Jean — a precious jewel from God."

I decided to stop talkin after I came to live at Woodlands — yup, jus stopped. That's cause it was bout the only thing the uniforms couldn't make me do. An sides that, when I was quiet the uniforms dint bug me so much. I guess I learnt that trick from Gramma. One time she said she wished she was a fly on the wall. And I said, "Gramma that's a funny thing to wanna be." She said if yer really small an quiet — like a fly on the wall — it was like bein invisible. You could hear what others was sayin but they dint bother you — that's cause they dint notice you was there. So after I stopped talkin the uniforms dint see me no more — nope, that's cause I was jus like a invisible fly on the wall.

But there was some days when I wasn't so quiet an invisible — nope, on account of a mean ball of anger squeezin me from the inside. Can't say zackly how I got like that — but sometimes I jus woke up in the mornin an there it was. Gramma called those days when you wake in a bad mood, "getting up on the wrong side of the bed." I guess that was my problem. I kept gettin up on the wrong side of the bed — cept I only had one side for gettin up on.

Then there was days I started out jus fine, but somthin bout the place made the meanness grow inside me. I could feel myself gettin madder an meaner through

the day till I was like a wound-up jack-in-the-box bout
to jump out at somebody. Maybe it was on account of
me not bein so smart. Or maybe it was on account of me
bein tired of waitin for somethin to happen.

All my days started the same. I'd be in bed, warm an
dreamin. My favourite dreams were bout snugglin tight
in Gramma's arms. She always hugged me a awful lot
fore she went to heaven in the amblance. But then the
lights on the ceilin would start to hum an crackle an jus
when they snapped on my Gramma dreams disappeared.
Those bright lights always hurt my eyes so I squeezed
em shut an tried to see Gramma gain, but it was too late
— she was gone. Then Millie would unlock the door an
come in — on account of she was day shift — an tell us
all to get oudda bed. Sometimes I dint wanna get oudda
bed so I turned over an tried to sleep some more.

"Come on, Ruby Jean. Don't give me any trouble
today. You don't want me to call the Boys, do you?"
I dint like the Boys — nope, not a'tall. If I dint cause
trouble Millie dint call em. But like I said, some days
I jus woke up with the anger inside me an it made me
cause trouble — yup, big trouble.

Some kids passed their time more peaceful than me
— yup, jus stared up at the ceiling, minds as blank as
the walls. Others looked oudda the window — maybe
cause they was hopin for someone to come for em. Then
there was the ones who watched TV all day. If Millie
was on shift we had the soaps — *Days of Our Lives* an *As*

19

the World Turns. Then jus fore lunch it was *The Price Is Right* with Bob Barker. But Bernice dint like soaps — so when she was workin we watched Julia Child's cookin show an *The Armchair Traveler.* I mighta liked to watch somethin different, but the TV was stuck at the top of the wall — way too high for me to reach.

When I was liddle I dint wake up angry — maybe on account of I got to go to the Woodlands school sometimes. That's where we was sposed to learn bout numbers an ledders. I dint never learn to read — but I learned to spell my name an count a liddle. School had books too with nice pictures of places an people — but none like the people who lived in Woodlands. Nother thing I liked was when Teacher let us count beans into a jar an sort bolts from nuts an screws from nails. She said it was important work. I dint understand how come after we finished sorting Teacher'd take those things an mix em all up again an give that important work to somebody else to do.

I liked school, but I dint get to go so much. Maybe on account of me not bein so smart … or maybe cause I was bad. Teacher use to complain to the uniforms, "There's just too many of them." Then I got bigger an dint go to school no more. That's bout when the anger got inside me for good. I can't esplain zackly, but sometimes after watchin beaudiful ladies an men on TV — an them eatin licious food, goin to parties an nice places — I'd start scratchin at myself. Yup, I jus wanted to hurt myself. I'd dig my fingernails into my skin, gougin an scratchin an twistin my hands till they was bleedin an sore — yup, awful sore. Uniforms said I did that cause I was bad. Maybe they was right bout that, but one thing's for sure — with fingers all sticky from blood an hands hurtin — the anger inside me got bigger. Uniforms dint understand bout me bein all hot inside. I spose times like that it was best nobody come near me — yup, best to jus stay away. But them uniforms dint knowed that — an if they started bosin me ... phew, I'd scream an scratch — an like Gramma said — I'd try like the devil to bite em. On days when I was bein really bad Millie or Bernice would yell for the Boys to come take care of me.

"I'm sick and tired of your crap, Ruby Jean!" Millie yelled one time when I was bein specially bad. I opened my mouth like a tiger an showed her my sharp teeth. "If you keep that up we're going to have the dentist yank your teeth out." I knowed it could happen cause Donald use to be a biter too an then he got his teeth pulled out — yup, every single one of em. After that the only time he had teeth was on vizzidin days when Nurse took em oudda the jar an put em in his mouth.

"I can hardly wait till I'm retired. Going to get my pension and get the hell out of this place — Lord knows I deserve it!" Millie screeched. Millie was mad that day, but I was awful mad too. I thought maybe I'd feel better if I could jus sink my teeth into her arm. It wouldn't be long fore the Boys came runnin down the hall so I took my chance an pounced on her. But I was too late. The Boys came through the door an throwed me on the floor. I tried to kick an bite em, but they had my arms twisted hind my back. It hurt a lot, but that dint stop me from bein mad — nope, jus made it worse.

"What is it with you today, Ruby Jean? Sometimes you sit like a vegetable, not talking, not doing a thing — now that I can take. But days like this, when all of a sudden you go nuts and start biting … well, I won't put up with it." Then she slapped me hard. "Take care of her, boys."

Sometimes when kids went berserk the uniforms tied em to their beds or put em in the bad kid room by themselves an left em there for a long time. But that's not what happened to me that day. Nope, that day somebody stabbed my arm an all of a sudden I felt sleepy — yup, so, so sleepy. Couldn't do nothin after that, next day neither.

Not all the uniforms was like Millie or the Boys. Sometimes we had priddy girls who came to the ward. I liked Rosemary lots … she brought a guitar an sang. I never bit Rosemary — nope, not a'tall. There was others too, but the good ones never stayed for long — like Marjorie.

One day Marjorie saw Peter slap me in the face. He slapped me cause I had a bad accident. Sometimes kids messed their pants to get the uniforms mad or jus to get some attention. But that day I dint mean to do it — nope, it was a real accident. I'd been waitin for everybody to get oudda the toilet room, but there was so many of em an they took so long. I jus couldn't hold it no more. I was even sorry I done it — til Peter slapped me an said, "You're a filthy girl."

That's when Marjorie came in an told him, "Stop hitting Ruby Jean."

"She's got to be punished — she deliberately crapped in her pants!" Peter yelled. I wanted to tell Marjorie it was an accident but she said it dint matter what I done. She said there was nothin I could do that'd make it okay for Peter to hit me. She told Peter she was gunna report him — yup, that's what she said. I guess Peter was fraid, cause he stopped hittin me. But I dint never see Marjorie again after that day. I heard Millie tellin some other uniforms she got sent to the laundry department for bein a big mouth. So that's why Marjorie had to go an how come Peter had to stay.

I missed Marjorie. She use to pet my hair an tell me I was a good girl. Wished she dint have to go away.

There was lots bout us Woodlands kids that was the same — yup, like we all had messy hair, wore clothes that was too big or too small an most dint smell so good. Some kids had eyes like little almonds, ears like a Misser

Potato Head, an fat tongues — some of em tongues was so fat they wouldn't stay inside their mouths. Then there was the kids who was so tired an slow they dint knowed there was drool runnin down their chins or snot drippin from their noses. Some of em had their arms tied round their selves all day long an rocked like wooden horses. Then there was the ones who dint look like retards a'tall — nope, cept for the messy hair an the smell.

There was the dangerus ones too. Uniforms said I was a dangerus one. Danny was too — cept he was only dangerus to hisself. He bit hisself sometimes, but a real bad thing he did was eatin cigrette butts. The Boys tried to stop him, but Danny was too fast — yup, on account of he could spot em cigrette butts far off an would be gettin ready. Sometimes he even snatched em from people while they was still smokin. Danny got lots of attention for eatin cigrettes — yup, lots more than when he dint.

Some people figured Woodlands School was the place the prime minister king man hid all of God's mistakes so others dint have to look at em. Maybe that's true. But I think us kids wasn't the only ones who was broken in that place — nope, some of em uniforms was awful broke too. I could tell cause they dint never look happy … dint smile … dint talk nice — not even to each other. Wondered if that's cause they dint like bein in Woodlands neither. Spose that's why it was a good thing they had families an places to go home to every night.

Summer was the best time of the year if ya had to live in Woodlands. That's cause we got to walk outside lots more an it was awful good feelin the sun shinin on me an the wind blowin my hair. An walkin those same paths year after year I got so's I knowed every tree an bush. They was all growin bigger — jus like me.

Sometimes we walked hind Willow Clinic where there was a nice, sunny park. My friend, Norval, told me it dint always use to be a park — nope, he said it use to be a place for the dead to get buried, a cemetery. His buddy, Willy Bennett, died long time ago an was buried there. Norval said he was sad for a long time after Willy died — yup, on account of he missed him a awful lot. Sometimes he got to vizzid the place they put him in the ground. But then Norval got sad all over gain when workermen came one day an dug up all those headstones with the dead people's names an took em away.

"After that I couldn't find Willie no more," Norval esplained to me. "Can't say for sure why those people took the headstones away. Maybe because of them sick people in the new hospital — guess they didn't wanna look out the window and see a sad old graveyard."

Nother thing Norval told me was how them workermen used them headstones for buildin a new sidewalk an for makin the uniforms a barbecue patio. "Maybe staff has to work real hard and need a place to relax," Norval said. "But I sure don't like Willy's name being covered in charcoals and barbecue sauce. No sirree."

Nothin Norval could do bout it — nobody cared what he thought.

One day Bernice took some of us outside to sit on the grass. There was some vizzidors walkin by — men in suits an ladies wearin lipstick. They smiled when they passed us. I heard some of what they was sayin.

"Dear God, this place is like a prison. And to think … their crime was being born with learning disabilities," said one guy.

Then the other man said, "It's crazy … some are here just because they can't walk, or have behaviour problems."

There was one lady who was kinda short — like me. She was all red in the face an sounded awful cross. "For too long disabled children have been left in places like this as though they were merely broken dolls to be tossed out with the garbage — and it's time it stopped."

I dint understand everythin they was sayin — I guess on account of me not bein so smart. Bernice must've understood, cause she said, "Fools!"

chapter 2

On good days the uniforms took us kids out to wander round the front garden — from there we could see the boats goin up an down the river an watch the trains screech an grind along the tracks. They'd sit on the bench smokin cigrettes an drinkin coffee, an leavin us be.

Bess part bout bein outside was the big sky an feelin the sun all over me like a warm blanket. Gramma use to have a sayin for times like that. She'd say she felt "free as a bird."

I liked birds. Maybe cause like Gramma said — they was free. But I think it was cause they was interestin an whenever I could I'd watch the birds round Woodlands. We had big ones with long necks that'd fly over us an sounded like a bunch of cars honkin in a traffic jam. Then there was the seagulls — they was the ones who'd say *squawk squawk squawk* an then poop on the windows. We had liddle ones too — cept they dint hardly ever sit still long enough to get a good look at.

The birds I liked best were the black ones — the crows. Yup, cause they sure was awful smart ... for birds. One day after it rained we went out in the yard. I stood still as a statue, watchin some of em. They mus have awful good eyes — cause they always knowed where to find the worms.

I watched one big ole crow — Mister Crow I called him — yank a long worm from outta the grass. Then he hopped over to a puddle with it — I guess so's he could wash off the dirt. I knowed that's what I'd do if I caught a worm — that's cause I dint like dirt on my food neither. That Mister Crow dint hop so good cause he had one foot all curled into a liddle ball. Then jus when he was bout to gobble that wrigglin worm a bunch of other crows came swoopin down on him. They started to peck and hit Mister Crow with their wings an screeched at him. When they finally flew away he was lyin crumpled on the ground.

I was sad cause I thought poor Mister Crow was dead. But after a bit he lifted his head an got up on his feet. He stood lookin round for a liddle while. Then he flapped his wings an hopped on that one leg of his over to the grass an began huntin for nother worm — yup, jus like nothin happened. When he got a good one, he hopped over to the puddle again. An jus like before, a bunch of em other crows flew down an beat him an took his worm. He layed there still as can be till they was all gone, then got up an went off huntin again. Yup, that happened over an over. Made me think it's not jus humans who got retards — crows had em too.

Finally, Mister Crow got hisself the biggest worm ever. But that last time he dint take it to the puddle. Nope, he jus gobbled that dirty ole worm right there on the spot. Then after a lotta wing flappin, he flew off oudda sight.

I wondered bout that ole crow for a long time — yup. An wondered why em other ones hit him an stole from him like that. Musta been lots of other worms round for them to eat. An nother thing — after bein beaten an stole from why'd Mister Crow keep tryin? Why dint he never give up?

A few days after a new kid came to live at Ward 33. I watched him comin down the steps into the garden holdin some lady's hand — maybe she was his momma. He had black hair — yup, black as Mister Crow. An a nother thing — he limped. That was on account of one leg was shorder than the other. That's what made me think maybe he was Mister Crow come back pretendin to be a boy.

He was havin one of those snifflin cries. But he stopped priddy quick when he saw us kids in the yard. He came over to us an had a good look. Then he smiled right at me. I dint smile back on account of me knowin that soon he was gunna be very sad. But for the time bein he looked real inerested in everythin round him — yup, made me member the first time I came to Woodlands.

His name was Jimmy. We already had a Jimmy on Ward 33. So the uniforms called him Jimmie T an the other kid got called Jimmy P — maybe on account of he sure peed hisself a lot.

The uniforms talked to the lady while Jimmy T was busy lookin round. She wiped her eyes a lot an then after a liddle bit opened her arms an Jimmy T ran for a hug. They was both cryin somethin terrible. Jimmy T tried to follow her out the gate, but the uniform's put their hands on his shoulder an wouldn't let him go.

An jus like I thought, there was a lotta cryin an screamin that day — an it only got worse an worse. That Jimmy T was priddy strong for a liddle kid — yup, lot stronger than me. After a while they threw him in the bad kid room. Us other ones listened all night while he kicked at the door an walls.

Then Morris said, "Get the Boys up here to shut this kid up." After that there was a liddle more ruckus — but suddenly everythin went quiet. Dunno why — but I cried after that.

We dint see Jimmy T the nex day, or the day after that neither. When he finally came in I hardly knowed it was him. No more nice boy clothes — nope, not a'tall. Instead he wore a baggy shirt that was long as his knees an big pants that bulged from the diaper he was wearin. His black hair was messy — jus like the rest of us — an his eyes was red an puffy. I knowed it was Jimmy T standin there — only it wasn't the same one no more. Nope, jus nother kid nobody wanted.

Nobody noticed him comin in the day room cept me — that's on account of em other ones was bein sleepy heads. Yup, the ones who liked to rock was rockin back an forth, back an forth. Some of the other ones was jus starin out the barred windows. An the ones who liked to watch *Days of Our Lives* on TV was havin a commercial break by their sponsors. "Tide Detergent: Look how it removes those unwanted stains and leaves everything smelling like spring."

Jimmy T came an sat down right nex to me. I dint look at him cause I was fraid of his sadness gettin inside of me. I knowed it was a long time ago that I was eight, but I still membered feelin that way — where yer good thoughts start slipin away an you can hardly member if you was ever happy. Me an Jimmy T sat side by side for a long time. Yup, sat together till the uniform came to check on him.

"How's it going Jimmy T?" said Uniform Roy. "Just give yourself time, little buddy. You'll get used to the place." I wondered how much time Jimmy T was gunna need, cause I'd been round for a long while an I still wasn't use to the place. The uniform patted him on the head an said, "You should come and meet some of the other little guys, Jimmy." He meant the ones who was huddled on the floor together, suckin their thumbs an wearin diapers. Gramma taught me how to use a toilet when I was liddle. But after Mom an Harold left me in Woodlands the uniforms made me wear diapers too. That's cause it's hard not to mess yerself when yer jus liddle … an lonely … an scared all the time.

After a few days Jimmy T got back some of his old self. An priddy soon he was kickin an bittin an messin in his pants jus like the rest of us. Only he was better at gettin those uniforms mad — yup, that's cause he was more like fireworks esplodin in the sky. But if he made too much trouble the uniforms called the Boys on him. Guess that's why he hardly got to go outside with the rest of us kids.

There was one time when Jimmy T did get to go outside with us. It was the day some kids went by — not kids like us — jus reglar ones. They was walkin by at the end of the garden. We could only see their heads on account of the stone-an-meddal wall bein so high. They was lookin at us an we was lookin at them. A couple of em ran away when some of us starded to walk over to em — maybe cause they was scared. But there was this one kid — he wasn't scared. Nope, not a'tall. He crawled up on the fence so's we could see him real good.

"Watch this," he said to his friends an then he put his thumbs in his ears an wagged his hands. "Hey, you bunch of flat-faced cauliflower ears — listen up.

> Two, four, six, eight,
> Keep the retards behind the gate.
> Watch them shuffle, burp and fart,
> Making smells right off the chart.
> Crazy, dirty, stinking bunch,
> Makes me want to lose my lunch."

Then the boy started laughin so hard he fell right off the wall. Some of us was laughin too cause he was priddy funny. Cept Jimmy T dint think so. Maybe cause he dint like bein called cauliflower ears. He was bout to run down to the bottom of the garden when a uniform yanked him by the shirt an put him in a headlock.

The other uniform yelled at them kids, "Get out of here before I come down there and knock your block off."

They all ran off, laughin an screechin like a bunch of old crows. I watched till their heads turned into liddle dots. When Jimmy T couldn't stop bein mad the uniforms had to drag him inside. Poor Jimmy T — he dint knowed lotsa people passed by like that jus so's they could stare an call us names. Can't say why they did that — they jus did.

One time I heard the uniforms callin Jimmy T a nutso. Maybe he was a crazy liddle boy, but I liked him that way. Yup, liked him a awful lot. An sides he made things interestin round Ward 33. If it weren't for him I wouldn't have had nothin else to do cept watch Maggie slap Lilly for kissin her boyfriend, Dr. Hughes, on *As the World Turns*. Nurse Millie said Woodlands' doctors dint never get priddy ladies tryin to kiss em cause they was all "a bunch of old balding war horses — wouldn't even make good dog food." Yup, that's what she'd say.

One mornin the uniforms was tryin to wash Jimmy T down in the tub room after he smeared hisself with custard he'd stole from the food cart. But somethin was different bout him that day. Even I had a hard time watchin him.

Poor Jimmy T — he'd been havin a lotta bad days that week. First he'd cut hisself with some broken mirror — had to get stitches on his face an his arm. Then he chipped his tooth from bangin his head on the wall. Then that mornin we could hear his angry screams all the way down the hall to the day room. Whenever one of us was actin too wild they stood us in the shower an sprayed us with the cold water hose. But that dint usually calm no one down … only made things worse.

So I guess it weren't no surprise that we could hear liddle Jimmy T screamin like the devil. But suddenly the screamin stopped and instead there was a loud crack — nope, not zackly a crack — maybe more like a thump.

Whatever that sound was, it made me member the time Bernice dropped the watermelon an it split open and the cafeteria floor was covered in red.

Dint hear no more screamin after that an Jimmy T left Ward 33 on a stretcher. Later I heard Millie tellin some uniforms Jimmy T got put in the special M ward — the one with the kids who couldn't never get oudda bed. "Poor little monster," she said. "He's a real vegetable. Won't be giving anyone any trouble now."

After that day the uniforms stopped callin the other kid Jimmy P an nobody ever talked bout Jimmy T again.

An I figured out Jimmy T was never really Mister Crow pretendin to be a liddle boy — nope, cause Mister Crow knowed he had to be patient to get what he wanted. He knowed sometimes ya jus hadda lie low an wait for that chance when em other ones wasn't lookin. Maybe if Jimmy T had been like that he'da got what he wanted one day — an jus like Crow, he could've flied away free as a bird.

chapter 3

One mornin Millie scrubbed me all clean an gave me a priddy pink shirt with liddle flowers to wear. I liked that shirt a awful lot — yup, that's cause it made me feel like I was a pink flower too. Then she combed my hair an sprayed it with sticky stuff so it stayed put.

"Ruby Jean, your hands are a mess," she said. "You've been scratching again, haven't you? Well, there's nothing I can do about that."

Sometimes I scratched my hands cause I was angry. Sometimes I scratched em on account of I got the jitters. Like the night before when the new uniform dint leave a light on in the hall. But there was lotsa things that made me jittery, like amblances an too many uniforms in my room at one time. But it's the dark that gets me jittery the most.

"There now, Ruby Jean," Millie said. "You don't look too bad. It's important that my girls look good when they go out. Right?"

I dint answer her, but I never did so she dint spect me to.

Millie took me down to the cafeteria an put a bib over me so I wouldn't mess my new shirt. Then she plunked down a tray with mushy prunes, porridge I knowed was gunna be cold, an milk I knowed was gunna be warm.

"You gave them Ruby Jean, eh?" Morris sniggered. "Mighty generous of you."

Morris was the uniform I'd bit most — yup, more times than any of the others. Partly cause I dint like him so much — but mostly on account of all the time he tried touchin me when I was liddle. He dint come so close to me no more.

"Should be fun to see what trouble she causes them snotty, save-the-world, life-skills workers," Morris said.

"We don't have it easy, so why should they?" Millie said.

"That's right. And it's our job to make them face facts that this bunch is no smarter than your run-of-the-mill mutt. Hell, some aren't even as smart as that."

Millie looked at me. "Well, that's probably true for most of them. But Ruby Jean — I think maybe she's got more going on in that head of hers than she lets on. Isn't that right, Ruby Jean?"

I dint answer her. But I never talked so she dint spect me to.

"It's her unpredictable behaviour that makes her a problem — and a perfect candidate for this program." Millie laughed.

I dint think much bout what Millie was sayin cause I was watchin Morris oudda the corner of my eye.

When I finished eatin Millie took me to the day room. Other kids were already there rockin an pacin an starin out the barred windows. Susan too. When the uniforms let me I always sat with Susan. That's cause she was my best friend. Norval Fontaine was my best friend too, but he got put downstairs when he got old. After that I only saw Norval when we was walkin outside. He always waved at me an said, "Hello, Ruby Jean. How's it goin?" I dint answer him. But I never talked so he dint spect me to.

Norval's favourite thing was watchin hockey on TV. When the Boys was round they always put the hockey games on. He told me one day he wanted to see a real-life hockey game. I sure missed Norval after he left Ward 33. That's cause he told me things — an even if I dint never tell him, Norval knowed I was listenin. He dint mind me not talkin anyways — that's on account of talkin was his second best thing to do after watchin hockey. I learnt lots of things from Norval, that's cause he could read an write a liddle an cause he'd been round Woodlands longer than anybody I knowed. He got left at Woodlands by his momma an poppa cause they was poor an cause he was a mental retard.

"They had to work hard to get enough money to look after my brothers and sisters, Ruby Jean. It wasn't their fault. After the doctor told them I was an imbecile and wouldn't amount to much, he said they should just put me in Woodlands so I wasn't a burden to the family. Sometimes my brother, Walter, comes to visit — brings me chocolate and batteries for my transister radio. And Vi always sends me cards at Christmas. Don't know what happened to little Ronnie and Elsa — I guess they're all grown up now."

Norval liked to listen to his radio in bed at night when the uniforms were busy. "I can hear music, and sometimes there's talking about important things — I don't understand so much of it. But I was listening the day they said a man was walking on the moon. Can you believe it, Ruby Jean — a man walking on the moon? I sure would like to walk on the moon one day. Wouldn't you?"

Susan was my other best friend, but she was like me — she dint never talk. Susan an me had been together on Ward 33 for a long time. Even though we dint say nothin to each other — I could tell if she was happy or jittery, an she knowed when I was bout to do somethin to make the Boys come. That's why she'd get up an move to the far side of the day room. But sometimes me an Susan was both jus fine an when that happened we sat holdin hands like sisters. I was glad I had Susan cause else I wouldn't have no one.

That mornin when I came in with my nice hair an priddy shirt Susan smiled so big. Then she touched my sticky hair an laughed. I sure wished Susan could get a nice shirt an sticky hair like mine.

"Sit here, Ruby Jean," Millie told me. "When it's time to go out, I'll come for you."

I sat on the green plastic bench nex to Susan an waited. I dint knowed where I was goin, but it dint matter cause I had a pink-flowered shirt an priddy combed hair.

After a while, a lady wearin shiny red shoes an dark pink lipstick came into the day room. I wondered if she was the one who was gunna take me out. But she dint look at me a'tall. Instead she walked over to Darlene who was starin out the window.

"Hello, Darlene. Say hello to Mommy."

Darlene dint look at Mommy. So Mommy took Darlene by the hand an tried to pull her away from the window. But Darlene dint wanna go an started moanin.

"Okay, okay," Mommy said. "Don't get excited. Let's just talk here by the window then. So how are you? Is everything going well?"

Darlene dint answer.

"Well, that's nice dear." Then Mommy pulled out a candy bar from her purse. "Look, Darlene, Mommy brought you something."

She dangled the bar in front of Darlene. I said to myself, if she doesn't take the candy priddy soon I think I will go over an get it myself. Finally, Darlene took the candy bar from Mommy, but she still dint look her in the eye. After a liddle bit Mommy kissed Darlene's cheek an patted her back.

"Well, dear, I'm off. I don't have time for a long visit today. I just wanted to pop by to say, hello."

Darlene's mommy never had time for a long vizzid — nobody comin to Ward 33 did. Even when her mommy was bout to leave, Darlene still dint look at her. Dint wave goodbye neither. She jus looked out the window an held the candy bar close to her till the uniforms came an took it away. Then she cried an messed herself. I wondered bout that candy bar — bout who was gunna get to eat it.

Mom an Harold use to vizzid me when I was liddle. One day, after I was at Woodlands for a while, they came to see me. Mom wore a white dress an she had a bracelet of flowers — maybe that's why she smelled like a garden too. Harold looked jus the same as always, cept for his shirt — it was clean an dint smell like cigars. I cried when I saw Mom.

"Oh, come on, Ruby Jean — don't spoil things. Harold and me came around so you could see how nice I look. Today's my wedding day, Ruby Jean. You should be happy for me."

I guess I was jus too liddle to care bout weddin days an dint knowed why I was spose to be so happy bout it.

I told Mom I dint like livin in Woodlands. "Please take me home," I begged her.

"I wish I could, Ruby Jean. But it's my honeymoon. Me and Harold are going to Reno for a while. Can't say when we'll be back."

Mom got one of the uniforms to take a Polaroid picture of us. When the picture was done Mom put it in my hand.

"Here, Ruby Jean. You have it so you can look at your pretty momma and new daddy whenever you like."

Mom dint come again for a long time after that. Then one day she arrived an had a baby in her arms. She told me that he was my baby brother. "His name is Harold, like his daddy." She dint look so priddy or smell like a garden any more. Instead her eyes were dark an that baby was spittin up brown stuff all over her. I dunno why I did it, but I hit the baby. I hit him as hard's I could. He screamed so loud I had to cover my ears. After that the uniforms came an pulled me down the hall. With the baby screamin an everybody yellin at me I never gotta chance to say goodbye to Mom.

I dint see Mom hardly ever after that day. I member she came once with a balloon an said, "Happy Birthday, Ruby Jean." That was the last time I saw her — mus be cause she was awful busy lookin after the baby.

"Ruby Jean … it's time to go out." Millie was standin side a priddy lady who had long red hair like Rosemary. "This is Grace. She's going to take you out for the day. She's going to teach you some new things. Are you going to be a good girl for her?"

"Hello, Ruby Jean," said Grace. "It's very nice to meet you." She reached out to shake my hand, but Millie pulled it away.

"I have to warn you — Ruby Jean's a biter." I got hot all over my face when Millie said that. "You never know what will set her off. One minute she's sitting peacefully, the next she's scratching and biting anyone within reach. I don't mean to scare you, but you have to be on guard with her."

"Thank you, Nurse. I read Ruby Jean's report and I'm aware of her history. But I feel confident that with the right stimulation we won't have any problems." Then she reached out to shake my hand. "Would you like to go out with me today, Ruby Jean?" I dint answer her. But I must've been smilin cause she said, "Great, let's go."

Me an Grace walked to the locked meddal door. Morris said, "Good luck."

Then Millie said, "Don't say I didn't warn you. And by the way, she's a runner too so keep a good hold of her."

Somebody started laughin down at the nurses' station.

Grace dint say nothin back. She jus looked at me an whispered, "We'll be fine, won't we?"

She unlocked the door an we went down the stairs that made the echo. I still liked to stomp my feet hard like when I was eight an came to Woodlands for the first time. But Grace dint squeeze my hand an say, "Stop it, Ruby Jean. Just stop it."

I was feelin awful good that day — yup, awful good. I guess cause I was dressed like a pink flower an had sticky hair an was outside takin a walk. Me an Grace walked for a long time. We walked passed the wards, an the rec centre, an passed the garden too. After a long while we got to a nice liddle brown house. In all my time at Woodlands I never saw that house before. It hadda front door — not a meddal one — an it wasn't locked neither. It dint look zackly like the house I lived in before I was eight, but it had a kitchen, a bathroom, an a nice room to sit in. I felt happy bein inside that house — yup, awful happy.

"This old house was where the B.C. penitentiary warden used to live," Grace said. "But now we've got it and I'll be bringing you here for training every day, Ruby Jean. You're going to learn how to take care of yourself. We're going to make sure you can wash yourself, brush your teeth, comb your hair — and even pick out your own clothes. Then when you're ready, maybe you'd like to learn how to make yourself something to eat — like toast, a salad, and maybe even how to make Mrs. Jiffy muffins. How does that sound?"

I dint answer her. But I knowed I was smilin cause I liked to eat an those Mrs. Jiffy muffins sounded awful licious.

"Good. Then let's get started," Grace said.

First thing Grace did was teach me how to wash my face an hands. Millie already done that fore she combed my hair an made it sticky. But I dint mind doin it again with Grace. That's cause she said I had to learn to do it for myself. She said there's a lotta things to member. First, I had to put the plug in the hole … then turn on the cold water an then the hot water. Grace said, "Don't let the water get too hot, Ruby Jean — we don't want it to burn you." After I made the facecloth wet I had to squeeze it. One time I forgot to squeeze. Grace said, "Never mind. Your shirt will dry." Nother time I forgot an got Grace wet. She said, "Never mind. My shirt will dry." Then I got soap in my eyes an it hurt a lot. I was moanin like the dickens but dint have no feelin to bite or hit. Nope, dint wanna do that a'tall. Grace told me, "Just keep practising, Ruby Jean. You'll get it."

After that Grace said it was time to go. I dint wanna go an wished I could stay in the liddle house forever.

"Ruby Jean, you've done very well today. I can tell you'll be able to learn many things in this program. Tomorrow we'll practise what you learned, then try some new things — like brushing your hair and teeth. Would you like that?"

I dint answer her, but I was smilin. What I was really wonderin bout was when I was gunna learn to make them Mrs. Jiffy muffins. Gramma use to bake muffins — blueberry oatmeal, an cranberry ones, an those peach bran ones too. They sure was awful licious.

The walk back to Ward 33 was too fast. Priddy soon we was stompin our way up the echo stairs an then we was back at my room with all the others. Millie was gone home so Grace talked to Bernice an Morris an told em all the good things I done. Then she said she would take me to the house again after one sleep. I was happy bout that — yup, awful happy.

When Grace left Morris said to Bernice, "I can't believe the little cretin behaved herself. Little Miss Do-Gooder's probably just too embarrassed to tell us how Ruby Jean acted up." Then he looked at me. "Did you bite her, Ruby Jean? C'mon, you can tell Morris."

Morris dint knowed I'd never want to bite Grace. Sure was gettin a feelin bout bitin him though.

Before I could eat, Bernice told me to take off my flowered shirt. "You can wear this again tomorrow if you don't mess it up. I'll put it in your bin, Ruby Jean." I hoped Millie wouldn't forget to give it back in the mornin. I wanted to wear the pink-flowered shirt every day. "Here, put this smock on for now."

Suddenly, there was a lot of bangin an noise comin from down the hall. A real commotion Norval would say. "Get a doctor up here quick!" yelled somebody. Whenever the uniforms called for a doctor I got the jitters — yup, everybody did. That's cause doctors comin to the ward was a bad sign. Jus then I thought bout Susan. I wondered if somethin bad happened to her. I sure dint want nothin to happen to my Susan

46

cause she was my best friend — yup, my only best friend after Norval left. When I went out to the hall I saw her watchin the commotion long with all the others. Seein her standin there made me feel bedder — but I still had the jitters.

"Okay, everyone, down to the day room," Bernice said. "Tom, you finish herding them down the hall and then stay there and watch them. I'll go see if I can help out."

Priddy soon I heard the whinin of a amblance outside. I had a hard time breathin after that an started scratchin at my hands somethin fierce. I dint like amblances — nope, that's cause they took people away an never brought em back. I think the other kids were gettin the jitters too — some were rockin an moanin, others was dartin back an forth cross the room like a bunch of dogs itchin to get oudda their cage. Susan hid in the corner an covered her ears. I tried to hold her hand tight — but she dint let me.

We had to stay in the day room for a long time. I got so hungry too — yup, so hungry my stomach started growlin. Susan musta been hungry too cause she started moanin — an from the bad smell I could tell she wet herself. It was dark when Tom finally told us to come eat.

Jus fore we went in to the cafeteria I saw the amblance men pushin somebody on a rollin bed. I dint knowed who it was cause of the big white sheet coverin him from head to toe. But I thought, oh-oh, whoever ya are, yer not comin back. I knowed that cause I'd seen others leave Ward 33 like that an never come back. Jus like what happened to Gramma — once the amblance got ya, ya dint never come back — nope, never.

I heard Tom talkin to nother uniform. He said, "The bosses must think we're a bunch of bloomin' magicians. Why else would they give us seventy kids when there's only five of us? Too many to look after ... hardly any training ... lousy equipment. Should be no surprise to anyone when they start dropping like dead flies."

I liked Tom — yup, he was one of the uniforms I liked best. But I never seen him do tricks so I sure dint think he was no magician — nope, not a'tall.

That night a bed got squeezed in nex to mine. Somebody's yellow-an-white pajamas was on top of the bed.

"You're going to have a new roommate, Ruby Jean," Bernice said. "Isn't that nice? Shirley's going to sleep beside you."

I dint understand why Shirley was gunna sleep side me. She liked to stay with Paulina. They was best friends — maybe even more best friends than me an Susan. After the lights went out, I heard a liddle voice in the dark. It was Shirley.

"Paulina's gone away ... won't come back. Poor, Paulina. Poor, poor, Paulina. Shirley said, 'Paulina, don't eat so fast. You'll get heartburn.' Then her heart stopped and they can't make it go again. Now they're gunna take

Paulina apart and give her away. Poor, Paulina. Shirley is sad, so, so sad. Ahh, poor, Shirley."

Shirley talked like that all night, but I dint mind cause she was sad bout Paulina. I was a liddle sad too, but mostly I was glad it wasn't Susan who went away in the amblance.

Sometimes I wondered bout dead people. Like, if no one got buried in Woodlands cemetery no more, where'd they put em? Norval told me bout that prison nex to Woodlands. He said, "There's a graveyard over there, Ruby Jean — at the penitentiary. That's where they bury the bad guys — the vermin and jailbirds. But they don't put names on their gravestones ... just numbers. That way nobody can tell who it is." Norval called em vermin an jailbirds — dint zackly knowed what that meant, but dint sound good.

Nother thing I wondered bout — after they buried em dead people — was what happened nex? Gramma use to say inside our bodies was our real self ... our souls. I knowed Gramma's real self got to go to the good heaven for nice people — that's cause she was a awful good person. But what bout Paulina an Willy Bennett an me? Did we get to go to the nice heaven or did we hafta go to the one for vermin an jailbirds and the retards? Spect that jailbird heaven's got barred windows an locked doors too. I sure wished I never had to go there — nope, don't wanna go to heaven if there's barred windows an locked doors.

Sometimes bein a fly on the wall's not such a good thing. That's cause sometimes I heard things I wished I dint hear. Like the night Morris told some other uniforms bout Paulina.

"Can you believe it — they dug out her brain and sent it to the medical school. Don't ask me why? I mean, what could they possibly learn from the brain of a halfwit?" Then he laughed.

I think Shirley heard him too an that's what upset her. That night in bed she wouldn't stop talkin bout it. "Poor Paulina, now she's dead, lost her head, can't get up in the morning. Poor, poor Paulina. Can't have a headstone cause she's got no head … nope, got no head. Shirley is so, so sad. Poor, poor Paulina." Yup, poor Shirley an poor Paulina.

After Paulina went away there was a lot more uniforms on Ward 33 — yup, a lot more — well, for a while anyways. Nothin happened like usual. For one thing — we all had to get oudda bed early. So that meant the porridge was warm instead of cold … the milk was cold instead of warm. The TV was off all mornin an we had nice music instead — the kind Gramma use to play on her record player. Nother thing — Grace dint take me to the liddle brown house.

"I'm sorry we can't go to the training centre right now, Ruby Jean. Nurse Millie says no one is allowed out of sight." Then she smiled big an showed me a box she brung. "Never mind. I've brought you some things to work on."

I wished we could go to that nice liddle house, but I was mostly happy cause Grace came to see me. I practised zippin zippers, an doin up buttons, an foldin towels, an makin my bed.

"Being able to do these things makes you independent, Ruby Jean," Grace said. "Next time we'll work on using a lock and key — something you're going to need to do if you're going to live in a house someday."

Live in a house someday? I couldn't figure what Grace meant by that. Sometimes she said things that got me mixed up — I guess it dint help with me not bein so smart. Still, bein confused with Grace was bedder than havin to spend my days watchin *As the World Turns*.

chapter 4

After the commotion settled down on Ward 33 me an Grace went to the brown house nearly every day. I got so good at washin myself an brushin my hair an teeth that Grace said Millie an Morris should let me do it for myself every mornin after I woke up an every night before I went to bed.

"Ruby Jean is really showing an amazing eagerness to learn," Grace said. "I'd say she's completely capable of taking care of her own personal hygiene, so please encourage her to practise."

Morris laughed. "Who'd of thought our little Ruby Jean was such an Einstein? Sharp as a tack, that one."

Grace frowned at him.

Then Morris said to me, "My, my, you can take care

of your own personal hygiene now. How wonderful is that?" He sniggered again.

I dint really knowed what those words *personal hygiene* meant, but when Morris said em it made me feel like I had a fire inside my tummy. But even if I had the feelin — I dint try to bite him.

"Oh, shut up, Morris," Millie said, laughing too. "Whatever they're doing together it's making Ruby Jean easier to handle. With her being in such a happy mood she doesn't have outbursts. In fact, she hasn't had an incident for weeks. And that makes my life a lot easier."

Millie was right. I was awful happy ... maybe as happy as when I was liddle an spent all my days with Gramma.

One mornin Grace came for me early when I was still eatin in the cafeteria. I wasn't finished my cold porridge an warm milk.

"Good morning, Ruby Jean. I'm glad I caught you before you ate too much. Would you like to have breakfast at the house this morning?"

I smiled as big as I could an she pushed my tray away. I looked to see what Millie would say. She was busy wipin Marsha's face cause Marsha put food all over herself. I think Marsha did that so's Millie'd give her attention.

I stood up an waited for a uniform to say, "Sit down and eat, Ruby Jean." But nobody even noticed me.

"What are you waiting for, Ruby Jean?" Grace said, smilin at me "Take your bib off."

I pulled off my bib an left it on the table side my porridge an milk. I looked again to see what Millie would say, but now she was snappin at Catherine for pushin her tray onto the floor.

"Damn it, Catherine, you got porridge all over my bloody shoes. Well ... that's it for you. You get nothing to eat until lunch. And it's your own fault."

Grace took me by the arm an led me away. "C'mon, let's get out of here, Ruby Jean."

I followed her down the hall with its polished green floors an matchin green walls. After Grace unlocked the meddal door I slipped my hand into hers. She smiled at me an squeezed it. I dunno why, but bein with Grace made me feel like maybe I was gunna laugh an cry at the same time.

Outside the wind was whippin everythin round. Grace had a ponytail tied at the back of her head so she dint mind the blowin. But my hair was flyin in my face.

"We should do something about your hair, Ruby Jean. You need something to keep it out of your eyes."

When we got inside the brown house there was a smell — yup, a awful good smell. It made me think of hot soup an soft, warm blankets on a cold day. Made me think of Gramma. I closed my eyes an took a big breath.

"Do you like that smell, Ruby Jean? I thought you would." Grace laughed. "That's fresh-baked bread. After I show you how to slice it we're going to make toast."

On the kitchen counter was a meddal pan with bread inside. It was round on the top an brown an I could feel it was still warm.

"Cutting bread can be dangerous, Ruby Jean. That's why I'm going to teach you how to do it safely. But first you need to wash your hands."

I walked to the sink an turned on the tap jus like I learnt. Then I rubbed my hands with the bar of soap an worked the soap into bubbles. That's when I noticed somethin — yup, I noticed all the sores on my hands were gone. There was still some old scars — but there was no blood an no scabs.

"Good job, Ruby Jean. Now I want you to make a gentle bridge over the bread with your hand, just like this."

Grace showed me how to hold the bread. At first I squeezed too tight an the bread crumbled.

"Okay, loosen your hand, Ruby Jean. When you're holding the loaf of bread pretend you're holding a kitten — ever so gently."

I tried to think if I ever held a kitten. Then I membered Gramma had a cat called Thomas. He was a big brown an white cat — looked like a tiger. When I was quiet an still he use to sit on my lap. He liked to be tickled under his chin an I made sure I was gentle when

I did that. I decided I would try to think of Thomas an not squeeze the bread so tight.

"That's perfect, Ruby Jean."

Grace showed me how to hold the knife in my other hand while she put her hand on top of mine. Together we pushed an pulled the knife — forward an back, forward an back, over the bread.

"There you go, Ruby Jean — a nice slice of bread that can be popped into the toaster."

Grace showed me how to take the toaster oudda the cupboard an plug it into the wall. Then she showed me how to put the slice of bread into it an to push down the handle. I tried to look inside to watch it toasting but there was hot air comin up into my face an I had to back off.

"The most important thing is to never put the knife into the toaster. That's very dangerous, Ruby Jean, and you could get hurt. Will you promise that you'll never do that?"

I could tell by the way Grace's eyes were starin into me that she was tellin me somethin important. I nodded my head so she knowed I promised.

Soon there was a licious smell fillin the kitchen, an that's when I suddenly membered somethin. I membered I'd made toast before. Yup, Gramma showed me long time ago. After a liddle while the toast popped up.

"Mmm, doesn't that look good? Take the toast out and put it on the plate." The toast was warm, even a liddle hot. "Okay, now what would you like to put on your toast, Ruby Jean — butter, jam, peanut butter — your choice?" I took the small knife off the counter an dipped it into the budder an spread it. Grace smiled. "Ruby Jean? You know how to do this, don't you?" Then I put the knife into the peanut budder jar an spread that over my toast too. Grace had a bigger smile. Then she laughed when I put the knife into the jam jar an spread some jam over top the peanut budder. "You're amazing, Ruby Jean. Look what you can do."

I broke my toast — some for Grace an some for me. We ate the toast together, but it was hard chewin with such a big smile on my face.

After that Grace let me do it again. I cut the bread … careful not to squeeze the kitten too hard … put the slice in the toaster … an then put budder an peanut budder an jam all over it. Then I got to eat it — yup, tasted so good it made my mouth awful slurpy.

"Ruby Jean, this is wonderful. I wonder how many other things you already know how to do."

Maybe Gramma taught me other things, but I had a hard time memberin. That's on account of it was so long ago when I was allowed to do somethin for myself.

"Would you like to make some tea now, Ruby Jean? I bet you'll find that easy to learn since you're so smart."

Suddenly, my face got all hot. I sure liked Grace — yup, a awful lot. But it weren't right for her to say I was smart. The uniforms, Mom, Harold, everybody — they all knowed I had to live at Woodlands on account of me not bein so smart. Like Morris said, "No smarter than your average mutt."

After me an Grace made tea we sat at the kitchen table to drink it. I wished I could've told her we needed more toast to go with the tea.

"Isn't this nice?" Grace asked. "Sitting here, drinking tea, far from all the noise. It won't be long, Ruby Jean, and you'll be ready to leave Woodlands — to live in the community."

Grace was doin it again — makin me get confused. Sometimes I dint understand on account of me not bein so smart, but then sometimes it jus weren't my fault a'tall. Nobody left Woodlands — cept on one of them rollin beds from the amblance. An I sure dint want that to happen. An besides that, if I left where'd I live? With Mom an Harold? I dint think that would be a good idea — I might hit the baby again an make him scream. Nope, I couldn't live no where cept Woodlands.

"C'mon, Ruby Jean. It's time for a little adventure. Let's go get something pretty for your hair."

Grace took my cup an put it in the sink. I followed her to the hall an we put on our jackets. Outside the sky was grey an the wind was blowin the trees round. But inside I felt like a sunny day.

She grabbed my hand an we walked down the hill — farther than I ever went before — toward the big stone-an-meddal gate. When we got there Grace pulled hard an the gate made a screechin noise that hurt my ears. I dint ever member goin outside the stone wall before — cept before Mom an Harold left me at Woodlands. Outside there was cars goin by this way an that — an goin real fast. Suddenly, I got the jitters an began scratchin my hands, but Grace took em in hers an looked me in the eyes.

"It's okay, Ruby Jean. You're safe with me. I promise."

We walked for a long time on that road with the loud noises an lotsa cars. One of em cars honked an that made me jump. Grace jus smiled an told me, "It's okay, Ruby Jean. You're safe with me." I wanted Grace to be proud of me so I tried not bein fraid.

After walkin for a while we got to a buildin with big glass windows an doors. Grace opened the doors — without a key — an we walked inside. I waited for someone to say — get her outta here, staff only. But no one said anything to me — jus stared.

That sure was a shiny place an there was lots of clothes hangin everywhere. I wondered who they belonged to. Somethin else — all em people walkin round was all strangers — dint see a single retard or uniform anywhere. But after a while I gotta funny feelin from em all lookin at me so much.

"Never mind the Lookie-Loos," Grace told me. She took my hand an we walked round that busy place lookin at shoes an sweaters an lady underwears. After that she said, "Let's go to the accessories department now and see about something for your hair." The accessories department was very shiny too — yup, it had bright lights an mirrors an lotsa priddy things.

"Hey, this looks like the perfect thing," Grace said. "Try it on." She pushed my hair back with a pink band. It made my hair stay up off my face so I could see bedder. "Take a look in the mirror, Ruby Jean."

I looked in the mirror. It was the same old me cept now there was a pink band on my head. I liked how it made me look an stared in that mirror for a long time.

"Don't you look pretty?" Grace said.

I had bubbles ticklin my insides so I laughed out loud. Then somethin unspected happened. "Looks priddy." At first I wondered who said them words. Then I looked at Grace an knowed.

"Ruby Jean! You said, it 'looks pretty.' You talked, Ruby Jean. That's … that's wonderful. Oh, my goodness, wait until I tell everybody!"

She danced round me an we both was laughin. My mouth sure got awful tired cause it wouldn't stop smilin.

After Grace gave some money to a lady we walked back hand in hand long that busy an noisy road to the screechy gate. An the wind dint blow my hair in my eyes no more — nope, not a'tall.

I thought bout all I'd seen an done that day — makin toast an tea, walkin long the scary road, goin inside the place with the clothes an bright lights. Somehow I knowed those things wasn't really new an strange

to me. Then words started poppin inside my head —
shoppin mall, grocery store, coffee shop, treats, gifts.
That's when a funny feelin got inside me an I felt like
I was liddle again, holdin Gramma's hand an walkin
home from Hudson's Bay with shoppin bags — some
of em even had things inside for me. When Grace an me
walked through the meddal gate I looked back an hoped
one day I'd get to go outside it again.

When we got to Ward 33, me an Grace stomped our feet
very hard when we walked up the stairs. The echo was
louder than ever before. We laughed too. Then Grace
put her arms round me an squeezed me tight. I had a
pain in my heart after that — cept it was a good one.

After we went through the locked meddal door,
Millie was standin there — waitin. Her arms was folded
an her eyes was skinny an mean. An I dint like the way
her lips was squeezed into a tight line. I'd seen that look
lotsa times before — like when I barfed up my porridge
one mornin. Millie said that day, "You did that on
purpose, didn't you, Ruby Jean?" Yup, I guess I done it
on purpose — but that's cause that porridge tasted awful
an made me wanna barf. But this time was different —
I'd never seen Millie look so mad at other people before
— the ones who weren't the retards. That's when I felt

the meltin inside me stop an everythin went hard again.

"Miss Watson, I just got off the telephone with someone who I consider a reliable witness. He told me you were seen outside the institution with Ruby Jean. He said you were walking along Columbia Street. Of course, I could scarcely believe what I was hearing. I thought to myself, certainly a young lady as intelligent as Miss Watson would not ignore procedures, disobey the rules. So please tell me that it wasn't true."

I watched Grace. She dint have no more smiles on her face. "Well, as a matter of fact we were walking along Columbia Street, Nurse. We went to the department store after Ruby Jean had a very successful morning — she made toast and tea and best of all she spoke. She said 'looks pretty.'"

"So you admit taking this patient off the grounds? And then you make up some fantastic story that she talked. In all the years I've known this girl she's never uttered a single syllable — nothing except the moans and groans these halfwits usually make."

Millie's face was gettin red an she was shakin so much I dint think she could hardly breathe. I wished I coulda told her that Grace was tellin the truth, but whatever it was that made me wanna talk before was all gone.

"Tell me — did you have written authorization to take this patient out of the institution?" Millie dint wait for Grace to answer. "Of course, you didn't. Ward 33 residents aren't allowed to go out in public unless there's specific permission — *spe-cif-ic per-miss-ion*. Get it? And I'm the one who gives permission. So what made you think you could just take Ruby Jean out without my permission?" Millie wagged her finger so hard at Grace I thought it was gunna fall off. "Well? What have you got to say for yourself?"

Grace's cheeks were shiny pink. I wondered if she was gunna cry. She'd never had Millie yell at her before. I waited for Millie to start callin her names too.

"You're right, Nurse. I didn't have permission to take Ruby Jean out. But I swear, she did talk." Grace's voice was awful small an shaky.

"Do you realize that if anything had happened to Ruby Jean while she was outside the institution we all could have lost our jobs?"

I knowed there's lotta things I don't understan on account of me not bein so smart. But one thing I knowed for sure was that I weren't so important as Millie said. That's why I knowed she was lyin to Grace — yup, jus like Gramma use to say, lyin her head off.

"I'm sorry that I didn't follow procedures," Grace said. "But, after all, Ruby Jean is in the life-skills program. We all hope one day soon she can be moved out of this place. She needs to get used to life beyond Woodlands, to know what it's like to live without locks and bars, to live in the real world."

Oh-oh. By the look on Millie's face I think maybe Grace said somethin real bad. I'd seen her face turn bright red like that lotsa times an knowed what Grace was in for now.

"How dare you suggest Ruby Jean hasn't been given the best life has to offer. How many can say they have a whole team of people lined up to make their meals, wash their clothes, clean their noses, and wipe their butts? Nobody — except maybe the queen of England!"

"I'm sure it's true that you all do a good job of looking after her physical needs, but Ruby Jean's more than just a body. She has a mind hungry for stimulation, a soul starving for affection. She wants to be useful and valued. And you don't need to be the queen of England to deserve all of that." Grace was shakin so much I thought maybe she'd fall down.

"First of all, you'll never teach this one enough for her to live outside this institution — so get that fancy idea out of your head. And second, your disregard for rules is going to cost you dearly — count on it. Ruby Jean, come with me."

Millie grabbed my hand an pulled me toward my room. I tried my best to keep my eyes on Grace, but they was fillin with tears. Before I knowed it she disappeared through the meddal door — jus like Mom and Harold when I was eight.

That night Bernice had to call for help. "Get the Boys up here again to handle Ruby Jean." When they came they grabbed my arms an twisted em hind my back. I was tryin to fight em off an that's when my pink hair band fell onto the floor. One of the Boys stepped on it an it snapped in two. That made me even madder — yup, almost as nutso as Jimmy T. I scratched an bit as hards I could, but priddy soon I felt a sharp pain in my arm again. Can't member what happened after that.

When I woke up the nex mornin I was lyin on the cold floor of the bad kid room. Millie came in — she had a bandage on her cheek. "So, Ruby Jean, I heard you were a bad girl last night too. Well, there's going to be none of that today. You hear? I don't have a problem calling the Boys again." I wasn't gunna be a bad girl that day cause I was too tired an too sad.

I waited a long time for Grace to come for me. It was hard waitin so I started scratchin my hands an made lotsa bleedin sores all over em. After a long time I went to bed, an after nother sleep waited for Grace again. But she dint never come.

When I was liddle an dint listen to Mom, she got angry at me. "You're a pain in the neck, Ruby Jean, and I'm fed up with you." After she said that lots an lots of times she an Harold left me at Woodlands. Guess I must've been a pain in the neck to Grace too — that's why she never came back.

Uniforms wrapped my hands in bandages so's I

couldn't scratch em no more. They dint do nothin for my sore heart — nope, guess they dint have bandages for that. I felt jus like a empty glass jar that had no jam inside. No more liddle brown house, no more toast an tea, an I was never gunna learn to make Mrs. Jiffy muffins. Stead I sat an watched *As the World Turns.*

After a while I started bitin the uniforms again. An when I couldn't do that I bit myself — yup, bit myself hard all over my hands, my arms, an anything else I could reach. I spose that's why the uniforms wrapped me up in a straitjacket an tied me down to a chair. That's when everybody turned fraid of me — even Susan wouldn't sit near me. That made me feel awful sad — yup, cause that's when I knowed I was all alone.

chapter 5

After Grace stopped comin I got more sad an more mad than I ever was before. I did my best to get the uniforms mad too — I messed myself, dint eat, an got so's I liked makin the others scared. But that dint last so long cause the uniforms started givin me the pills.

The pills made me awful sleepy — yup, so sleepy I couldn't do bad things no more. Alls I could do was sit in a chair all day an drool. Couldn't walk, dint wash myself, dint brush my hair or dress myself neither. I was jus like a baby again.

When I was liddle I had a pet turtle named Herman. I membered Gramma use to laugh at Herman an say, "Ruby Jean, that turtle is the doziest creature I've ever seen. He's just sleepwalking his way through life." That's bout what

I was like — a sleepwalkin turtle. Yup, like Gramma used to say, "Eyes wide open, but there's nobody home."

Some days I had imaginations — like bein in the brown house … that Grace was there … sometimes Gramma too … an we'd be eatin toast an drinkin tea. I like havin those imaginations. But night was different. I was tied to my bed so I wouldn't bother nobody and with that feelin gone away — all I could do was think … an wish. I was awful sad — yup, so sad I sometimes moaned an cried all night long. Times like that all I wanted was for the uniforms to give me more pills or maybe even one of those shots in the arm.

One mornin fore they gave me pills, I heard Millie talkin to Morris an Bernice outside my door. I pretended I was asleep so's they wouldn't bug me.

"I don't know what else to do. I can't go on drugging her like this forever. On the other hand, I can't risk having her attack us again, right?"

Then Morris said, "Damn right — keep her doped up. She's not the only one we've got to look after, for chrizesake."

Gramma dint like that kinda talk — she used to say anyone who cussed out the name of the Lord was a trash mouth — yup, that's what she said, trash mouth.

"That's easy for you to say," Millie said. "You don't have doctors checking records, asking why her meds have tripled. And after thirty years in this place the last thing I need is for some doctor to accuse me of not doing my job right. I can't risk anything interfering with my pension."

I wondered what a pension was an why Millie was fraid of losin it.

Bernice told em, "I know what you mean. Dr. Bonehead called me last night too and wanted to know if anything unusual happened to Ruby Jean to cause her to start biting again. I didn't know what to say to him."

"Those lab coats like to think they're on top of what's going on over here in the wards," Morris said. "But if the truth be told they really don't know a thing and don't want to know — nobody does. We're the only ones who know what's really going on. That's because we're the ones who have to shove these halfwits out of bed every morning, hose 'em down, feed 'em, and then park 'em down the hall just so we can get ready to do it all over again after lunch."

Bernice laughed. "Morris, you make it sound like we're running a factory assembly line and these kids are just a bunch of mugs that need to be stacked on a tray or widgets to be packed in a box."

"Anyone who cares to be honest about it knows that's just what they are. And when one of those widgets balls up the works it has to be fixed or dumped."

"Morris, stop!" Bernice said. "That's callous — even for you. But honestly, Millie, if you've got doctors calling up and poking around, you've got a problem. You need to figure out how to fix this."

That day I dint get no pills. Instead I got tied to a chair and was awake all day long. The nex day too. Then one mornin I saw Millie lookin at me through the liddle window on the locked door. "Good morning, Ruby Jean," she said after the lights snapped on an the door opened. "I have a surprise for you today." I dint forget bout what Millie done to me an Grace, an wasn't in no mood to listen to her.

"C'mon, don't you want to know about your surprise?"

Millie pulled off my blanket an tried draggin me outta bed. I mighta liked to jump up an bite her nose off, but instead I jus rolled over.

"Ruby Jean Sharp, if you get up and get yourself ready, you'll be able to go out."

I looked up at Millie — she was smilin. Nope, I said to myself — I dint wanna get up — jus wanted some of em pills so's I wouldn't be sad. An maybe if I was lucky I'd have some of em nice imaginations too — imaginations of bein with Gramma an Grace at the liddle brown house or maybe I'd be goin to the big store to look at all the shiny new things.

"I promise it's something you'll like." Millie tried ticklin me, but I jus buried my head deeper in the blankets. "You like going down to the training house and learning how to take care of yourself, don't you? How would you like to go there today?"

The liddle brown house? Grace? I rolled over an got oudda bed awful quick — yup, so quick I wobbled an nearly fell down.

"Not so fast, Ruby Jean. It's been a while since you've been up on your feet."

The air in the room made me shiver an the floor was icy cold too. But I couldn't help smilin — yup, jus like Gramma use to say, I was smilin from ear to ear. Millie dint give me the pink shirt with flowers to wear, but that dint matter. Grace was comin an we were goin to the liddle brown house.

Millie let me wash my own self an comb my own hair. Then I followed her down to the cafeteria for breakfast. I was so happy I couldn't sit still an tried eatin fast as I could. I wondered if me an Grace was gunna make toast an tea or maybe I was gunna finally learn to make Mrs. Jiffy muffins.

"What's with this one today?" Morris asked. "Looks like you gave her a shot of the happy juice."

"Ruby Jean?" Millie said. "Oh, she's just excited because she's going to the training house."

"Good. Let's hope that fixes her. Like I said, if the widget's happy, she won't ball up the works." Morris laughed. "And you know what that means? It's business as usual — wake 'em, hose 'em, feed 'em, park 'em ..."

"All right already," Millie said. "I get it."

I was used to bein called things like moron, idiot, an even retard, but I sure dint like bein called a widget, even though I dint knowed what that was. Gramma once told me somethin bout sticks an stones can break my bones, but names don't break my bones. I think she meant I shouldn't care bout what Morris called me — cause I knowed I wasn't a widget ... even if he said so.

After eatin my cold porridge an warm milk an prunes — it mus have been Monday, cause we only got prunes on Mondays — Millie took me to the day room to wait. I watched a lady win a new car on *The Price Is Right*. She was so happy bout it she started jumpin round an huggin Bob Barker right there on the TV. That made me laugh, cause I was feelin like that too an wanted to jump up an down an hug somebody. That's when Susan came over an sat nex to me. She held my hand tight. Maybe she did that cause she missed me as much as I missed her.

Millie came into the day room a liddle later with a grey-haired lady. I never seen that lady before, but she made me think of Gramma. She had a grey button-up sweater that matched her hair, an shoes Mom use to call "all business." But what I liked best bout her was them liddle eyes — they was laughin an sparklin all at once.

"Ruby Jean, this is Mrs. Gentry. She's come to take you to the training house." I looked up at the smilin lady. Then I leaned over to see hind Millie — to see where Grace was at.

Jus then Millie put a leash on my wrist. "Ruby Jean's had some behaviour problems lately, but she should be okay now … we hope." I got hot in the face when Millie said that. "She was acting out, attacking staff, so we sedated her to keep her under control. But she likes going to the training house, so I don't expect her to give you any trouble. Just in case, though, when she's outside this building she's to wear this leash at all times. Do you understand?" Mrs. Gentry nodded an took the end of the leash from Millie. That's when Millie looked at her up close. "When I called for a new life-skills worker for Ruby Jean, I was expecting someone … well, frankly, someone younger. Are you sure you can handle this?"

Mrs. Gentry laughed. "Not to worry, my dear, not to worry."

"Well, Ruby Jean can be a quite a handful — aggressive, uncooperative — like that," Millie said. "And if she doesn't want to do something, you can talk till you're blue in the face and she still won't comply. Believe me, I've tried. And if that temper of hers flares — be careful." I got even more hot in the face after Millie said that. "You let me know if she gives you any trouble."

"Thank you, Nurse, for your concern. What I've discovered is there's always a way to reach people. We just need to be patient, kind, and find the key that unlocks their hearts and minds."

Millie laughed an said, "Whatever. Just don't let her get away from you. There's no telling what she might do.

Don't get me wrong, but if you ask me giving Ruby Jean the idea she's got what it takes to live on the outside ... it's a pipe dream. But, hey, at least it keeps her happy and off the ward — so knock yourself out." Jus then Jillian started peein in the corner. "See what I mean? They're like animals. Jillian, you bad girl!"

Mrs. Gentry turned to me an smiled. "Well, shall we go, my dear?"

I followed Mrs. Gentry to the locked door. I was glad to be goin to the liddle brown house, but I dint feel much like stompin my feet down the echo stairs. I jus followed along quietly. I sure dint like wearin that leash neither. Made me feel like a dog bein walked round the block — made my arm sore too. As we walked Mrs. Gentry dint chatter away like Grace used to. But she sure did smile an hum a lot.

When we got to the liddle brown house I wondered if it would smell like fresh bread inside or if there were flowers in the vase, or if the teakettle was waitin by the stove, or if Grace was there. But there was no smell of bread or flowers an no Grace. Soon's we was inside Mrs. Gentry took the leash off my wrist an dropped it on the floor.

"There now. Let's get rid of that blasted leash. It's not the kind of thing a young lady wears — is it, Ruby Jean? Ah, well, never mind. Say, I hear you enjoy a good cup o' tea and can make it yourself." I noticed somethin was different bout her voice — it dint have the same sound as other people. "My late husband, Harry, used to say the day didn't feel right till he had a good cup o' tea under his belt."

Mrs. Gentry handed me the kettle. I turned on the stove an then put water in the kettle. After that I put the kettle on the hot stove an took out two tea bags, two cups, two saucers, an the teapot — jus the way Grace showed me. Soon's the kettle whistled I poured the hot water into the teapot. Grace said her grandma was from a place called England an they always warmed the teapot first fore makin tea. So I dumped the hot water into the sink an filled the teapot again. After that I put the tea bags in the teapot.

"Well, now, someone's taught you the proper way to make a good cup of tea. I thought it was only us Brits who made it that way. Very nice, Ruby Jean. Very nice, indeed."

That day Mrs. Gentry taught me to make a garden salad. First, I washed the ledduce like she said an tore it into liddle bits. Then she showed me how to cut carrots an tomadoes an cucumbers jus the way they did on the TV cookin shows. It was a beaudiful salad — an tasted awful good too. Afterward I washed the dishes an Mrs. Gentry dried em.

When we walked back to Ward 33 Mrs. Gentry dint put the leash on my arm. Stead we walked hand in hand. A liddle way fore we got back we stopped.

"Ruby Jean, dear, I'm going to ask you for a favour." Gramma used to call me dear. "Just so we don't get in any trouble from the nurse I'm going to ask you to put this darned leash on. I'm sure you don't like it — and I don't either." I dint always think so good, but I knowed what Mrs. Gentry wanted. I held out my arm so's she could put the leash on. "Ah, what a dear girl you are. Grace told me you were a real sweetheart."

Hearin Grace's name made me a liddle happy an a liddle sad too. I secretly wished it was her walkin side me stead of Mrs. Gentry.

When we got back up to the ward Millie was gone home, but Bernice was there. She took the leash from Mrs. Gentry an unbuckled it. I rubbed the red mark on my arm.

"So how did it go?" Bernice asked. "Any trouble with her?"

Mrs. Gentry smiled. "No, there wasn't a spot of trouble — from Ruby Jean or from me." Mrs. Gentry winked at me. "So shall we do it again tomorrow, luv?" I smiled — maybe not so big a smile like with Grace — but I liked goin to the liddle brown house an learnin things too. "I'll take that as a yes then. Good. See you tomorrow, my dear."

I watched Mrs. Gentry leave an jus fore she went through the locked door she turned back an waved at me.

After that Mrs. Gentry took me to the brown house almost every day. I learnt lots of things — like how to tie my shoelaces an lock an unlock the front door of the liddle brown house. I learnt how to boil apples into applesauce an make soup from a can. An then Mrs. Gentry showed me how to use the TV an telephone. I learnt bout dialling 911 too — an how a nice lady would get me the police man, or the fire man or the amblance man. Cept I dint never want the amblance man to come — nope, sure dint want that.

Funny thing bout learnin — it made me wanna think all the time. I still dint knowed much on account of me not bein so smart — but I had a feelin maybe I could learn to be a liddle smarter — specially if people like Mrs. Gentry helped me.

Millie was happier too cause I dint bite any more an the doctors stopped askin her questions bout me. After a while she said I dint have to wear the leash. Nother good thing happened too — Morris got sick an stayed away for a long time. Gramma used to tell me that jus cause I dint like somebody I still shouldn't think bad thoughts bout em. So I thought a good thought bout Morris — like how it was good he was sick an had to stay away.

Nother thing started happenin — the days got longer an the sun got hotter. Then the trees got leaves an the new flowers started pokin up from the dark ground. Mrs. Gentry showed me how to pull weeds from the garden an taught me some names of flowers too. The yellow ones with the liddle cups were called daffodils. An the ones that looked like tiny purple stars were periwinkle. An my favourite was the big flowers that looked like pink fireworks — rododo somethin.

One mornin I was sittin in the day room with Susan, waitin for Mrs. Gentry to come get me. The TV was on like usual — *As the World Turns* was jus gettin started. Dr. Hughes was still mad at Jessica for pushin his wife into the swimmin pool. But I wasn't interested in none of that — nope, cause I was busy thinkin. Thinkin bout lotsa things, like how many eggs you gotta have for makin pancakes, an why some plants are called flowers an others called weeds, an what happens if you put in more than one cup of laundry detergent into the washin machine, and what tastes bedder on toast — strawberry jam or honey. Nother thing I was thinkin bout was how I still wanted to learn to bake Mrs. Jiffy muffins an how I liked bein in the liddle brown house better than on Ward 33.

With all that thinkin I was surprised when I looked up an saw Mrs. Gentry an Millie standin right front of me. Side em was two guys — lab coats, Morris always called em. One of em was short as me an had no hair. The other was skinny an had lots of hairs — mostly inside his nose an ears.

"Doctors, this is the girl," Millie said. "Ruby Jean, get up. You're coming with us today."

Nobody was smilin so I got fraid I was in big trouble. I started to twist an scratch my hands. But Mrs. Gentry touched my shoulder an whispered, "Nothing to be afraid of, dear."

Millie held my hand an took me downstairs to a big room. It had the same green floor as Ward 33, but the walls was pink instead. An there was a big table in the room with lotsa chairs. Millie told me to sit at the end. She and Mrs. Gentry sat on one side an the doctors sat on the other.

"Ruby Jean, I'm Dr. Lennox and this is Dr. Martin. We're here today because Mrs. Gentry has submitted an application on your behalf, requesting that this institution consider you a candidate for placement in a community setting. During the course of this interview, we intend to determine whether you're ready for such a major step."

I had a hard time followin the doctors' words on account of me not bein so smart — an on account of me bein busy watchin his long moustache go up an down like a little hairy critter stuck on his lip. Gramma used to call moustaches cookie dusters, but I never could think of why anyone would wanna dust their cookies.

"After this interview, we'll evaluate your case, come up with our recommendation, and provide our response to this request," Dr. Lennox said. "So are you ready to begin?"

I still dint understand an looked over at Mrs. Gentry for help. Her eyes looked like I never seen em before — dark as a stormy winter day.

"In less highfalutin words, what the doctor means, Ruby Jean, is we're going to have a friendly talk about the things you've been learning, how happy you've been lately, and if it's a good idea for you to move out of Woodlands and into a home."

I smiled at Mrs. Gentry. Her words made lots more sense. For a long time she'd had a idea that I should leave Woodlands an live someplace else. At first I dint believe that could happen, but I was startin to get the idea maybe I really could leave one day. When I looked at Dr. Lennox his face had turned splotchy red.

"Ah, thank you, Mrs. Gentry. Now shall we begin?"

We was all in that liddle room for a long, long time. Mostly, Mrs. Gentry, Millie, an Dr. Lennox did the talkin. The other doctor did lots a writin on paper. Dr. Lennox sure asked lots a questions bout me. Millie told bout all the bad things I done an Mrs. Gentry told bout all the good things. But with all that talkin my eyes dint wanna stay open for long — nope, I got sleepy an full of imaginations.

I had a nice dream that I gotta wear a pink-flowered shirt every day. An I made toast an tea for breakfast cause that's what I wanted to eat — not cold porridge. Susan an me went to the store an I bought her a pink band for her hair. Then we vizzided Norval an brought him muffins I made by myself. In my dream nobody told me what to do — I got to do whatever I wanted …

"Ruby Jean, are you listening?" Millie asked.

Oh-oh — I wasn't listenin a'tall. I looked up at Millie whose eyes was small an narrow again.

"For heaven's sake, wipe the drool off your lip, girl, and sit up." I rubbed my mouth on my sleeve an tried to listen bedder. "The doctor needs to know if you can do what you're told." Millie looked at the doctors. I wondered if they knowed bout me not bein so smart. "Don't expect much. This patient can be quite uncooperative."

"Well, if that's the case, then we're all wasting our time, aren't we?" Dr. Lennox said. "But, on the other hand, if these reports are accurate, I'd say we should see what Ruby Jean has learned in the program and whether she's capable of learning more. So let's get started, Mrs. Gentry."

"There's nothing to be concerned about, Ruby Jean," whispered Mrs. Gentry. Then she said out loud, "Now, Ruby Jean, would you please untie your shoes and take them off."

I dint knowed why she asked me to do that. But I always did what Mrs. Gentry asked me too — that's cause I liked her ... an cause she liked me too. I pulled apart the laces on both my shoes an loosened em. Then I pulled back the tongue jus like I was sposed to do an took em off my feet.

"That's wonderful, dear. Now, if you don't mind, will you show us how well you can put them on again and then tie your laces?"

Mrs. Gentry was bein silly. Yup, awful silly — first she asked me to take my shoes off an then to put em back on again. But it dint matter if it was silly, I did what Mrs. Gentry asked.

In my head I said the shoelace song she taught me: "Criss Cross an under the bridge, gotta pull it tight. Make a loop but keep a tail, that is how to do it right. Then I take the other string, wrap it round the loop. Pull it through the peepin hole, now you've got the scoop."

"That's all very well, Mrs. Gentry," Millie said. "But being able to tie her own shoes doesn't mean she's equipped to live outside Woodlands. Quite frankly, I find this all —"

Dr. Lennox shushed Millie. "Please continue, Ruby Jean." This time it was Millie's face that got splotchy red.

After that I showed em how I can button up buttons an zip zippers an tell red from pink and blue from green. I used the tatoe peeler to take the skin off the tatoe, an cut a carrot into little bits. Finally, Dr. Lennox told me to use the telephone to call Mrs. Gentry. I dint think that was a good idea cause she was sittin in the chair side me, but I dialled her number anyways. Course I knowed she wasn't gunna answer the telephone — nope, not a'tall.

After I did all em things everybody stopped payin attention to me an started talkin between themselves. Dr. Lennox said stuff like "cognitive power" and "supervised independent living" and "societal risk." An

Mrs. Gentry talked bout "nurturing environment" an "freedom to grow."

Millie jus kept sayin, "It'll never work. It'll never work."

All that talkin was jus makin me sleepy gain. The only thing I knowed for sure was Mrs. Gentry was tellin em all I should leave Woodlands an live in a house. Not Millie. She said, "Ridiculous."

"Thank you, Ruby Jean, for your patience," Dr. Lennox said. "And thank you everyone else for contributing to this meeting. Dr. Martin and I will take some time to review everything we've learned here today and come up with our recommendation."

When Dr. Lennox was finished talkin, Millie took my hand an we started to leave the room.

"Oh, Nurse, before you go, can you tell us why this girl is mute?" Dr. Lennox asked Millie.

"Nobody knows why, Doctor. She just stopped talking soon after coming here."

"I see. Well, if she's going to cope in the community, she'll need a way to communicate her needs. This might be a problem."

"That's something I intend to work on with her, Dr. Lennox," Mrs. Gentry said. "From what her previous life-skills worker reported, she was just beginning to speak again. I believe it's an issue of trust."

Millie huffed loud an rolled her eyes at Mrs. Gentry. "Ruby Jean hasn't spoken a word in all the years I've known her. And I wouldn't believe a thing the previous worker had to say. After all, she was fired. If you ask me, the chances Ruby Jean will ever talk are about as likely as a bunch of monkeys learning to sing."

I looked up at Mrs. Gentry. She jus smiled an winked at me. "We'll see," she whispered in my ear.

chapter 6

"Time to get up, Ruby Jean. Today's the big day." I wondered why Bernice was wakin us up an not Millie. That morning the room was so full of sunshine we dint even need the big ceilin light. "Come on, everyone. Shirley, you too. Time to get up."

Shirley rubbed her eyes an sat up an looked at me. "Poor, Ruby Jean. Poor, poor Ruby Jean. First Paulina went dead, and lost her head and couldn't get up in the morning. Now poor Ruby Jean going away today. Shirley is sad, so, so sad. Poor Shirley."

"Oh, hush, Shirley," Bernice said. "Paulina didn't lose her head. And besides, Ruby Jean might not like living out there — away from Woodlands and all her friends. She might come back — right, Ruby Jean?"

I dint answer Bernice, an she dint spect me to. But if I did talk I think I would've told her I'm gunna try real hard to never come back to this place — nope, never.

Three sleeps ago, Dr. Lennox came to Ward 33. He sat with me an Millie at the long table in the meetin room. He told us the doctors said it was okay for me to move oudda Woodlands on a try basis — that's if I behaved. I think he was sayin if I dint hurt myself or others I wouldn't have to come back. Millie told him he was makin a mistake.

"We have patients much more capable than Ruby Jean." I guess Millie said that on account of me not bein so smart. "Besides, Ruby Jean is much too unpredictable."

"Well, it was you who chose Ruby Jean for the independent living program," Dr. Lennox said. "Were you just trying to sabotage it?"

"Of course not. I just didn't think they were actually going to put one of my kids out there."

"It sounds like you not only underestimated the goals of the program, but you underestimated Ruby Jean," Dr. Lennox said.

Millie dint answer the doctor, but her face got red as tomadoes.

After Dr. Lennox left, Mrs. Gentry came to see me. She told me I would be livin with Mr. an Mrs. Williams. She said they had kids, but the kids were all growed up. They was a gramma an grampa too. I liked that — never had a grampa before.

"This is going to be a wonderful new life for you, Ruby Jean. But I want you to know it's not going to be easy. There's a lot for you to learn, things that will seem strange and scary to you. And people — well, not all of them will accept you. Some will be afraid, others will just be plain old mean. That's because they don't know any better, dear. But we're going to change that, right?"

After I got up that mornin Bernice put a small box on my bed. I opened the top an looked inside an saw some folded clothes. "Those things should do you until you get more." I was happy cause the pink-flowered shirt was in the box. Then Bernice unlocked the small drawer inside the closet with my name on it. "You'll want to take these things too."

I smiled so big when she brought out Barbra. I nearly forgot bout my best old doll. Her head was nearly bald an her priddy dress ripped cause of all em days an nights I held her tight. After I got bigger I guess I stopped needin her so much. But jus cause she was bald an dirddy dint mean I'd stopped lovin her. I hugged Barbra tight an then put her into the box carefully.

There was other things in that drawer I dint member I had — a wallet with no money, a cup that said RUBY JEAN, an liddle pine cones I got from the park where Willy Bennett got buried. All em things I put into the box nex to Barbra. The nex thing Bernice pulled oudda the drawer made me clap my hands — it was the golden locket Gramma gave me jus fore she went to heaven in the amblance. I opened the liddle door an inside was a picture of me an her in our back garden. I was eight the last time I saw my locket — that's cause we dint wear jewellery at Woodlands. Bernice put the locket in my box with Barbra. Finally, Bernice took some pictures out. Fore she put em in my box she let me look at em.

I smiled at the one of me an Gramma sittin by the Christmas tree. I membered that time real good. Then I looked at the other pictures — there was Mom an me sittin on the couch at Harold's office … one of me standin side of Mom an Harold on their weddin day — they was holdin hands an smiling, but I had tears in my eyes … an the last one was of Mom an baby Harold.

I took the picture of Gramma an put it in my box. The other ones I put back inside the drawer an closed it.

"We're ready!" someone shouted from down the hall.

"All right, time for breakfast, Ruby Jean. Come on, Shirley, you too."

I followed Bernice down to the cafeteria and wondered if I'd be eatin cold porridge an warm milk at my new home too. When we walked in to the room people shouted, "Surprise!" Yup, that's what they said — "Surprise!" All of em Ward 33 kids were smilin an wavin. Susan was there an some uniforms too, like Tom an Roy an Bernice an Dr. Martin — Mrs. Gentry too. They all looked happy. I looked round the room but couldn't see Millie nowhere — she was day shift an supposed to be there.

All round the cafeteria was balloons an a big sign. Bernice told me it said GOOD LUCK, RUBY JEAN. I could tell the part that said Ruby Jean.

"We wish you all the best and hope you'll remember your friends back here at Woodlands," Tom said when the kids got quiet. "We have a little going-away present for you."

He put a box on my lap. It had a pink bow on top an the paper was shiny. I loved my present an held it tight. I used ta get presents from Gramma — but that was a long time ago.

"C'mon, open it, Ruby Jean," Tom said.

I dint want to open my present cause it looked so priddy jus like it was. But the people was all sayin, "Open the present, open the present." So I decided if I was real careful I could take the paper off without tearing it.

Then Morris came over an said, "My toenails grow faster than this. Here, let me help you." Then he tore my present open an threw my shiny paper on the floor.

I dint bite no more, that's cause I hardly ever got mad. But when Morris tore my paper an throwed it on the floor I sure hadda feelin I wanted to bite him. But I dint — nope, jus had a big feelin bout it.

The box on my lap had a picture of shoes. I thought it was sure nice to have new shoes. But then I opened the box an there was no shoes inside — nope, no shoes a'tall. Instead there was other things — like a mirror, a hairbrush, a toothbrush, an a new tube of toothpaste all for me, an a liddle bag to hold all those things. There was some coloured paper an pens too an a box of candy.

At the bottom was two more small presents wrapped in priddy paper. I took the paper off the first one quick an put it on my lap so's Morris couldn't rip it. Inside was lots an lots of things for my hair, like clips, an ribbons, an hair bands — a pink one, a blue one with bows, an two white ones. None as priddy as the one Grace gave me, but I was happy cause they was mine for keeps.

I opened the second present. It was a picture of all us Ward 33 kids — yup, it had me an Susan an Norval an the others too. I membered that day — the day we were all smilin for the camera. It was summer an there was a big celebration. We all got to eat hamburgers an cake an wish Canada a happy birthday. I membered that day, cause we was happy.

I never had a party jus for me before — a party with presents an laughin. My face felt awful warm, jus like my insides. I only wished Grace an Gramma could've been there to see me so happy — an I dunno why, but I wished Millie was there too.

Priddy soon it was time to hug my friends goodbye. Shirley wasn't happy that I was goin. She said, "Poor Ruby Jean. She's going away, going away like Paulina." But then she got happy when I gave her one of my white hair bands.

At last I said goodbye to Susan. I looked in her eyes an could tell she looked happy for me. I hoped she would get oudda Woodlands one day too ... maybe come live with me and the Williamses. I opened my shoebox an handed her my pink hair band — that's cause it was the priddiest. She laughed when Bernice put it on her head.

"Well, it's time to go, luv," said Mrs. Gentry.

As we walked long that hall with the polished green floor an matching walls, Mrs. Gentry held my hand. It was a good thing too cause I was feelin nervous an a liddle wobbly on my feet. Some of em kids patted me as I walked away. I had a last look inside the rooms with the barred windows and meddal beds. Funny thing bout that ... I could see myself in em rooms an I was eight again.

I turned an waved to everyone down at the day room. Just when I was bout to go through that locked meddal door for the last time I saw Millie. I waved, but she dint wave back — nope, just watched me leave.

As we walked down the echo stairs I membered the first time I came up em. I was holdin Mom's hand — she scolded me for makin so much noise an said, "Stop it,

Ruby Jean. Just stop it." Now, after a long long time, there I was all growed up, holdin hands with my friend, Mrs. Gentry, and goin back down em for the last time.

As we drove down the road I had a strange feelin inside of me. Somehow the place dint look so bad from the inside of a car — a car that was leavin. When we drove passed the big stone-an-meddal gate I looked back an watched as everythin got smaller an smaller. It weren't till Mrs. Gentry handed me a tissue that I found out I had tears runnin down my face. Dint knowed why — cause I sure was awful happy.

Drivin in a car was like bein a balloon — I felt all light an bouncy as I watched all em trucks an cars an buses an bikes goin this way an that. An passin by so many buildins too — there was some big an some small, an some was department stores with people goin in an out, an some was jus liddle places with only one or two inside. When we drove cross a bridge I saw the river below — there was a tiny liddle boat draggin a big box filled to the top — wondered how somethin so small could be so strong. Soon we was passin lotsa houses an grassy places where liddle kids ran an played. Even if everythin looked new an different, I knowed I'd seen it all before.

"Here we are, Ruby Jean. This is the Williamses' place and your new home." Mrs. Gentry drove her car up in front of a white-an-green house an stopped. I dunno why but all of a sudden I had the jitters an started twistin an scratchin my hands.

"Now, Ruby Jean, we've talked about this. You don't need to be afraid. These people are wonderful and they're looking forward to meeting you. Please don't scratch yourself. Everything will be okay — you'll see." Mrs. Gentry was awful good to me an I knowed I could trust her. So I tried real hard not to scratch my hands. "Okay, ready? Let's go meet your new friends."

We went up to the front door an Mrs. Gentry let me push the button. I was surprised to hear a bing-bong sound comin from inside the house. When the door opened I saw my new friends for the first time. I can't esplain it on account of me not bein so smart, but the second I looked at em I knowed everythin was gunna be okay.

Mr. an Mrs. Williams said I should call em Nan an Pops. I dint call em that cause I dint talk, but I wanted to. Then Nan told me to follow her down the hall.

"Here's your bedroom, Ruby Jean," Nan said. "We did our best to make it beautiful. Do you like it?"

I dint member seein walls that weren't green, or windows without meddal bars. In that room — the room Nan said was mine — the walls were yellow with tiny flowers an the window had fluffy white curtains.

An the bed — instead of brown meddal an a mattress covered in plastic with green sheets — it was white an big an soft an had a frilly skirt that looked like it was sposed to be for a princess. There was a big pink chair with pillows, drawers with shiny handles, an pictures on the walls of horses an flowers. Suddenly, I was one of those happy ladies on *The Price Is Right* that won the big prize an I felt full of bubbles an Jell-O. There was a rumble inside me an I laughed — yup, I laughed out loud. Nearly scared myself. That's cause I dint knowed I could laugh like that.

The day Mom an Harold left me at Woodlands was the saddest day of my life — yup, saddest day of all. But that day … the day I stood in my new room … in my beaudiful new house … with my new family — that was the happiest. Yup, cause I was finally home.

chapter 7

The first night in my new home I couldn't sleep — nope, not a wink. In the corner of my room was a small light that made everythin orangcy — Nan an Pops put it there cause Mrs. Gentry told em I dint like the dark.

"There are things that make Ruby Jean nervous, like being in the dark, the sound of ambulances and crowded places," she told em. "Try to keep these things in mind as you help her to adjust to her life outside the institution."

But even though I had a night light an was awful tired, I still couldn't sleep. I dint know why till I figured it out — it was cause it was way too quiet in my room. Yup, I was used to lotsa noises ... like voices down in the office ... an the buzz of the big lights in the hall ... an the clink of meddal locks an doors. An

I was used to sleepin sounds from the kids in the beds nex to me — sleeptalkin, snorin, cryin. I layed there in my new bed, wishin I could sleep. But wasn't no use — jus too quiet.

After lots of nights like that I started to nap in the day while Nan banged round the kitchen … or vacuumed the house … or talked on the phone. She dint mind cause Pops liked to nap like that too. Then one night Nan put a radio side my bed an left it on. Priddy soon I was goin off to sleep listenin to Kenny Rogers an Dottie West an Ronnie Milsap an lots of others too. After that I slept like a baby. Sometimes when I listened to them guitars an sad songs I wondered bout Norval — wondered if maybe he was lyin in bed listenin too.

One thing I liked best bout livin with Nan an Pops was how the house smelled. My room smelled clean — not a'tall like Lysol. More like flowers. An the bathroom smelled like a garden too, even after … ya know … big business. But the kitchen smelled the best … like liciousness. That's cause Nan was a awful good cook — yup, awful good.

Nother thing I liked bout my new home — I could help Nan cook. She said I was good at choppin vegables an stirrin the pots. But the best part was when we baked — Pops always got to lick the spoon an I got the bowl. I never knowed a bowl could taste so good.

Mrs. Gentry came to see me a lot. One day she brought some pictures. They was nice pictures … of food … an people walkin in a park … of a man sleepin in bed an lots more.

"We need to find a way to help Ruby Jean begin communicating with us," Mrs. Gentry said. "For now she could use these pictures to tell us things. If she wants to go outside for a walk, she could show us this picture of people walking. Or if she wants to help plan meals, she can tell us by choosing from these food pictures."

I looked at the pictures of all the things to eat an boy oh boy, I suddenly got hungry — hungry for spaghetti an pie, soup an buns, salad, apples, an muffins!

"I hope one day Ruby Jean will begin talking again," Mrs. Gentry said. "We know she used to when she was little. But that's not likely to happen until she feels completely safe. So for now these pictures will be a good way for her to start. Right, Ruby Jean?"

I smiled as big as I could at Mrs. Gentry.

"Let's try it out," Nan said. She spread the food pictures all over the counter. "Okay, Ruby Jean, tonight's your turn to pick supper."

I looked into her smilin eyes — I could always tell bout Nan by her eyes.

"Nan, this is a new experience for Ruby Jean." Mrs. Gentry said. "She's never been asked before about what she wants. It might take her some time to get used to it."

I looked at all em pictures an my mouth got slurpy — yup, awful drooly. There was macaroni, hamburgers, spaghetti an chicken. Everybody laughed cause I took so long.

"Sorry, Ruby Jean, can't have it all tonight!" Nan said. "But you can pick one."

After a long time all that decidin got me jittery. I jus couldn't pick so I started scratchin my hands. But then Pops helped me an pointed to the macaroni.

"How about some good old macaroni and cheese?" he asked.

I membered Gramma used to make that. I smiled an put my hand on the picture of macaroni.

Nan smiled. "Mac and cheese it is! Don't worry, Ruby Jean, dear. It'll get easier."

After that Nan an Pops used those pictures all the time to help me make decisions. They'd put em out on the table an say, "What would you like to do today, Ruby Jean?" Or "Which of the chores do you want to take on — dusting, folding laundry, drying dishes?" Or "It's Friday night, Ruby Jean. What will it be? A movie, maybe a puzzle ... how about dancing?" Thinkin bout dancin with Pops always made me laugh.

Then one day Nan told me it was time I started makin my own breakfast. "There's lots you can prepare by yourself, dear. Of course, there's toast and tea. But you could get yourself cereal, fruit, put some waffles in the toaster ... lots of things. And on special mornings we'll cook eggs or pancakes together. Okay?"

I mostly jus liked to make tea an toast for breakfast,

but sometimes I had other things too.

When Nan first told me I should make my own breakfast, I started havin it all mornin long — right on till it was time to start havin lunch. Nan was surprised when the bread kept disappearin so fast.

"Pops, I just took a loaf of bread out of the freezer last night and it's already finished," she said one day. After that I think she musta figured out I was havin more than one toast an tea. "I see you like to eat, Ruby Jean. But if you don't watch out you're going to start packing on the pounds. How about from now on you have breakfast only once each morning?"

I liked to eat on the sundeck on nice days an look down on the liddle orange fish swimmin in the pond. Those goldfish swam round an round an round that liddle pond. Made me think of Jessie an Melinda an Susan an all the others on Ward 33 — jus like the liddle fish, they was goin round an round in circles, nothin changin, nowhere to go. Then I got a idea ... the idea was to drop a bit of my toast into the pond jus to see what the fishies would do.

At first they bobbed up an down tryin to decide bout that toast. When they finally figured it was somethin innerestin, somethin good, they all crowded round an wanted some of it. When it was gone they jus went back to swimmin round in circles. That got me wonderin what'd happen if I dropped other things into the pond. So one time I dropped in a piece of my nutloaf. Nother time it was potato chips. An once it was a piece of chicken — cept now I knowed fish dint like to eat chicken.

One day Pops came into the house an he was mad — yup, awful mad. "Something's been killing those goldfish — I found another four of them belly up this morning. And the pump and filter are all gummed up with greasy gunk. I wonder what's causing it." After that I only gave the fish small bits of toast — yup, jus once in a while.

Tea use to be my favourite drink fore I tasted Nan's mint hot chocolate. Nan made it for me one night an after that I wanted it all the time. Nan said I had to be careful bout all the sweets I was eatin an drinkin … said I was gunna get fat. But I dint think I minded bein fat a'tall — specially if I could have mint hot chocolate every day. Pops dint care bout bein fat neither. He always said, "Let's celebrate, Ruby Jean!" Then he'd get out the cookies or Licorice Allsorts. Nan frowned, but she dint never really mind.

One time I decided to make myself a big cup of mint hot chocolate — cept it was in the middle of the night. Nan an Pops was sleepin so's I was quiet — yup, quiet as a mouse. After I had two cups I got sleepy an went back to bed. But I woke up later an my bed was wet — yup, all wet cause I peed in my sleep. I was fraid what Nan would say, so I hid the wet sheets an my pajamas in the closet. The nex day Nan came into my room.

"Oh, dear, it smells awful in your room, Ruby Jean. Something's gone bad … what could it be?" All morning

I'd been hearin Morris inside my head callin me a retard. I guess I thought Nan would be mad at me too.

When she finally found the smelly things in the closet, she said, "Ah, I see, Ruby Jean. Did you have an accident?" I dint look in her eyes, cause I dint wanna see her angry. "Accidents happen, dear. C'mon, let's put these in the wash. I'll show you how to do it, then next time if you have an accident you can fix it all by yourself. Okay?"

After that I only had mint hot chocolate at day time — never at night time. Nope, dint do that again. But if I had an accident I wasn't so fraid of what Nan an Pops would say. Could still hear the uniforms in my head though — yup, couldn't get them to stop callin me names.

I liked doin things with Pops a lot — yup, bedder than havin breakfast all day long or drinkin mint hot chocolate. That's cause he was fun — he liked celebratin — an he taught me lotsa things too.

One day he told me, "You're going to be a working girl soon, Ruby Jean." He said I was gunna get a job at Four Leaf Shelter Workshop an even get money. After that he showed me how to put stuff together — like light switches an a birdhouse, an flower boxes too. At first I dint do a good job cause I couldn't member all the things he told me to do. But Pops dint get mad at me — nope, he jus kept tellin me again an again an again.

One day I heard him talkin to Nan. "It took me a while, but I finally figured out the secret to teaching Ruby Jean."

"What's that?" Nan asked.

"The secret is to not talk too much."

Nan laughed when he said that. "Well, I could've told you that."

"Very funny. But seriously, Ruby Jean's a visual learner, and when I try explaining things to her it's like the words confuse and distract her. But if I simply show her how things work, she watches carefully … then, man, look out. Last week I told her how to assemble the light switch — I told her over and over and she still couldn't do it. Then yesterday I just showed her — didn't say a word, just put the pieces together. I did it once more just in case she'd missed a step. Then, by golly she put that thing together without a hitch. It was amazing!"

"I know what you mean," said Nan. "I've never seen anyone put puzzles together as fast as she can. I guess she just has a knack for seeing how things fit together."

Pops an me went walkin every day. Sometimes we went round the block an sometimes we went to the park. I liked goin to the park best cause there was liddle kids there. I liked playin with em in the sand or pushin em on the swings. Some of the mommas was scared of me an so they took their kids home. But some of em dint mind an let their kids stay an play with me.

If Nan wasn't at home waitin for Pops an me, we went to Harvey's Doughnuts for a snack after our walk. After that Pops would pat his tummy an say, "Nothin like a nap after a walk and doughnuts, eh, Ruby Jean? C'mon, let's go home." Then me an Pops took a liddle nap while Mr. Cronkite talked on the TV.

My real favourite thing to do with Pops was shoppin at Spencer's Grocery. Pops an me went shoppin every Tuesday. That's cause he said that was customer appreciation day an the best time for sales. I dint know nothin bout customer appreciation till I started grocery shoppin at Spencer's with Pops. They got ladies givin out yummy samples an coupons too.

Pops said ya gotta have a system for grocery shoppin — that's why we always started at produce. Fore goin to Spencer's I dint knowed that fruits an vegetables could look like rainbows — yup, a rainbow you could eat. They got orange oranges, green an red grapes, yellow squashes an bananas too, an there's peppers that come in yellow an orange an red an green. An boy oh boy — they got apples in all sizes an colours too.

It was my job to push the grocery cart. Up an down we went puttin lotsa food into the cart — milk an cheese, eggs, bagga flour, cereal, frozen juice, frozen peas. An boy oh boy — there was the potato chips an ginger snaps an so many kindsa crackers. Finally, we'd go to the bakery department — the best part of shoppin. While Pops went to find bread on sale I got to look inside the glass case at all the tarts an squares an cinnamon buns. Lookin at them goodies always made my mouth get all slurpy.

There was one thing I dint like bout shoppin — nope, dint like it when people stared at me. Can't say why I was so interestin to em.

"Never mind them, Ruby Jean," Pops told me. "You'd think by the look on their faces you were from Mars."

I wondered where Mars was. Maybe one day I was gunna go there an find out if I really did look like them people that come from there.

One time when Pops an me was in the bakery department I stood nex to two boys who was pickin out a big cake. We was all there lookin at the good stuff to eat. Then one boy started whisperin to his friend — cept he weren't too quiet cause I heard what he said.

"Gawd, take a look at that — it's a retard. Man, they give me the creeps."

My face got all hot an my heart hurt too — yup, felt just like heartburn. I tried to think why some people dint like me. All I could say was maybe if I was more smart I wouldn't like me neither. Then I membered that silly boy on the fence — the one who called us kids flat-faced cauliflower ears — the one Jimmy T wanted to get.

I walked away from them boys an followed Pops to get fresh bread.

"Try not to feel bad, Ruby Jean," Pops said. "Some people just don't know how to accept others who are different."

Pops went round the bakery getting all kindsa bread — brown bread, white bread, raison bread, an even some nut bread. When those two boys walked passed with their cake — an boy oh boy, that cake looked licious with all that chocolate icin an red flowers on top — Pops stopped em.

"Hi there, fellas," Pops said to the boys real friendly. "I'm Pops Williams and this here is my friend, Ruby Jean." The boy in the green shirt went splochy red like Dr. Lennox. "I overheard you back there, and I just thought I'd take the opportunity to tell you a little something about my friend here." Then Pops told em boys all bout me — how I liked to listen to country music, an how he'd never knowed anyone who put a puzzle together fasser than me, an how I was learnin how to do hook rugs with Nan, an how my favourite thing to eat was toast an tea. "I just thought I'd tell you all that because folks usually aren't so afraid of someone once they get to know them."

"I ain't afraid, old man," said the boy. "Retards give me the creeps — didn't say they scared me. Anyway, you should mind your own business. Didn't your momma teach you that listening to other people's conversations wasn't polite?"

Pops laughed. "You got a point there, son. Thanks for the lesson on etiquette. Ruby Jean and I are just trying to do our best to fit in, be good, and live a happy life."

The boy said, "Whatever."

Then he walked away. I dint think he liked me any bedder after what Pops said. But jus when those boys turned the corner, the other one looked back an waved. "Bye, Ruby Jean."

One mornin Pops said, "Today's the day you start working at Four Leaf Shelter Workshop, Ruby Jean."

"You can help me make your lunch," Nan said.

I got confused on account of I dint have my breakfast yet. After we finished makin sandwiches I sat down to eat em.

"Not yet, dear. This is for later." Nan put the sandwiches in a brown paper bag. I sure was glad when she asked, "Okay, now what would you like to eat for breakfast?"

A liddle later Mrs. Gentry came an got me. When I was gettin in her car Nan called out, "Now don't eat your lunch until it's time, Ruby Jean. It's a long day and I wouldn't want you to get hungry."

It was too late — I was already hungry jus thinkin bout the cheese an cucumber sandwich, oatmeal cookies, Granny Smith apple, an tin of orange juice sittin on my lap.

When me an Mrs. Gentry was driven to Four Leaf, she told me bout the place. "I guess you could say it's like a training centre for people like yourself, Ruby Jean — people with disabilities. But after training at Four Leaf, many of the clients go on to jobs in the community and earn a good living. Some work in factories, restaurants, grocery stores — lots of places." Mrs. Gentry talked bout the job I was gunna do. Then she said, "And you're going to earn a little pocket money too, Ruby Jean. You'll have to start thinking about what you'd like to do with it. Maybe you'll want to save it — that means opening a bank account."

I dint knowed bout bank accounts an I couldn't think what I would buy with money — cept maybe get me nother pink hairband. Maybe I could give some of that money to Susan an Norval.

There was lotsa people like me at Four Leaf. They all said hi to me — some patted my shoulder an hugged me like they'd knowed me for a long time. Supervisor Audrey was a nice lady an told a boy named Ronald to show me my new job — makin flower boxes. I was secretly glad I already knowed how to make em — Pops showed me.

"Ooookay, Rrrrruby Jean, I'm ... I'm gunna show ... gunna show you how to make a flower box. Ooookay?" Ronald stuttered.

I watched him carefully. He gotta small cardboard box an walked passed the table an picked up four pieces of wood — two long pieces an two ends an a bottom —

then put em in the box. Then he picked up two meddal strips an some tiny nails an put em in the box too. After that he took out a liddle hammer and started puttin all em pieces together — almost same like Pops showed me.

"Ooookay, Rrrrruby Jean, it's … it's yourrrr turn."

I did everythin jus as Ronald showed me — it was easy.

"How ddddo you like that ffffor apples? That's ppppretty gggoood, Rrrruby Jean. You … you surrrre are a smart girl."

I liked Ronald, but he dint knowed me so good — nope, he dint know I'm not smart a'tall.

I made lots of flower boxes that mornin. Then a bell rang an everyone stopped what they was doin an left their work stations.

"Cccome on, Rrrrruby Jean — it's lllunchtime," Ronald said, then smiled.

I membered the food I brought in the brown bag an was glad Nan dint let me eat it.

I liked workin at Four Leaf — liked it a lot. I made new friends an they liked me jus the way I was. Mrs. Gentry came back later an drove me home. "So did you have a good day, Ruby Jean?" I smiled as big as I could. "That's good. Would you like to go there tomorrow too?" I clapped my hands cause I really wanted to go there again.

When we got home there was a blue car in the driveway. I found out it belonged to Greg — that's Nan's and Pops's boy. When I came in the house, he shook my hand until it nearly fell off. "It's nice to finally meet you, Ruby Jean. Mom and Dad have told me lots of good things about you. Are you getting used to the place?"

I dint answer him, but I smiled as big as I could.

"I can see how you'd be happy living here with Mom. But Dad — well, he's just a crazy old man. You'd better watch out for him." Then Greg did somethin bad to Pops — he hit him in the arm. But Pops jus smiled.

I dint think Pops was crazy an I sure dint like somebody hittin him — even if was his own son. I felt like a pot of Nan's bubblin hot soup bout to boil over the top. I decided I dint like Greg — nope, not a'tall.

It'd been a long time since I'd such a bad feelin — a feelin of bein angry enough to hit an scratch. I started twistin an poundin my fists like one of those TV wrestlers. That's when everybody stopped talkin an looked at me.

"Ruby Jean, what's the matter, dear?" asked Nan. "What's upset you? Something's upset Ruby Jean. I've never seen her look so angry."

Then with em all jus lookin at me it happened. "Nooooo hittttin Pops." The words came oudda me slow like a guard dog growl. Everybody looked awful surprised. Then I said it again louder, "Nooooo hittttin Pops."

Pops laughed a liddle an said, "Oh, Ruby Jean, Greg and I are best friends. He was just teasing me. When we do that it's just playing."

Playin? I dint understand that kinda play. In Woodlands the only time people hit each other was when they was mad or bein mean.

"Wait a minute here — Ruby Jean's just done something quite amazing," said Mrs. Gentry. She looked me in the eye. "Ruby Jean — you spoke. We know what you're feeling because you told us — that's wonderful, dear."

I dunno what was so wonderful bout me feelin like a angry bull bout to knock Greg over. But priddy soon they was all laughin an dancin round the kitchen. Pops an Mrs. Gentry were talkin citedly, and Nan was singin, "No hitting Pops. No hitting Pops. Ruby Jean says, 'No hitting Pops.'" I dint think Greg was so happy cause I was still lookin at him oudda my squinty eyes.

After that day, whenever Greg came over to our house, he'd say, "I know, I know — no hitting Pops." I dint get mad no more when he an Pops played their hittin game ... but I still thought hittin was a awful way to play.

Nother thing bout all that was Nan an Pops always tryin to get me to talk. "I can't decide what to have for supper, Ruby Jean. What should we eat?" Nan'd ask. If I dint say she would wait an wait an wait — till my tummy growled.

An Pops would say somethin like, "We're running out of milk. I wonder what we should do about it?" If I dint tell him we had to get more milk I dint get my tea. Fore long I was talkin every day. Always sounded funny hearin em words comin oudda my own mouth though. Seemed like they was really comin from somebody else.

I sure had a lotta happy days livin with Nan an Pops — yup, awful happy days. Then one afternoon I came home from Four Leaf an everythin was changed. I could tell the minute I came in the house — a feelin … not a good one. Greg was there with his arm round Nan. I saw her eyes was like puffy cherries. She tried smilin at me, but it wasn't a real smile — nope, not a real smile a'tall. I wondered why Pops wasn't round.

She wiped her nose. "Here's our Ruby Jean. Dear, there's something we need to tell you — something about Pops."

Suddenly, I felt like somebody was pressin down on me an I couldn't hardly breath. I dint even knowed what she was gunna say, but my neck got all stiff an my stomach got jittery.

"Pops isn't here, Ruby Jean."

I looked at her shiny nose an red cheeks an the box of tissue in her hand. "Pops gone away in a amblance?" I asked her.

"Yes, Ruby Jean. They took him away in an ambulance."

After she said that I ran to my room. Nan came an knocked on my door.

"Ruby Jean, honey, we need to talk."

I dint want to talk. "No, Nan!" I cried. "No more talkin." Jus like Gramma, the amblance took my Pops to heaven. Nan tried to get me to come out an eat supper with her an Greg, but I was too sad. I dint want to eat an dint want to talk neither.

Liddle while later I heard Nan go out an she dint come home for a long time. When she did I listened at my door to her an Greg talkin in the livin room.

"It's best if you don't have Ruby Jean to worry about right now," Greg said. "I'll call Mrs. Gentry in the morning so she can make the arrangements."

Worry bout me? Make arrangements? I dint want to go nowhere — nope, jus wanted to stay with Nan … at our home. I don't member cryin so much in all my life — nope, not since Mom an Harold left me at Woodlands when I was eight. No more grocery shoppin at Spencer's with Pops, no more cookin with Nan, no more happy home for Ruby Jean. I cried so much I dint even notice when I fell asleep.

chapter 8

I stood in the day room lookin through the glass-an-meddal bars at the dark grey sky. I waited for Mister Crow to fly by but he wasn't nowhere round. Maybe he stayed way cause he could feel the awful sadness comin outta me. I tried hard to hide it by tellin myself over an over, "Ruby Jean's invisible. She's like a tiny fly on the wall." But it was hard bein so tiny an quiet when my hands hurt so bad from all em bloody sores. "Don't let em see ya like this or they're gunna call the Boys," I tole myself. Dint wanna get a needle or tied to a chair neither — nope, not a'tall. "Shush, Ruby Jean. You be okay if you don't make no moanin or cryin noise and stay here in the corner."

Good thing the uniforms had too much work to do — too many bums to wipe, kids to feed, no time for nonsense. "We've got to wash 'em, dress 'em, feed 'em, park 'em," said Morris. "Then get ready to start all over again."

Bernice laughed. "Might as well be mugs on a tray or widgets packed in a box."

"Watch out for that one — she's a biter," Millie said. "Biters should have their teeth pulled out. That's the only way to fix them."

I dint wanna, but I started cryin. I cried so much I surprised myself. Yup, that's cause I suddenly sat up an found out I weren't in Ward 33 a'tall. I was jus in my bed havin a bad dream — yup, jus havin a very bad dream. Funny thing bout that — even if it was jus a dream my heart was zoomin like a race car an I had a awful feelin Morris was standin there, lookin down on me.

"I promise I won't bite no more," I tole him. "Please don't pull my teeth out."

Then I heard Shirley in my head. She was sayin, "Poor Pops. Poor, poor Pops. Now he's dead, lost his head. Ruby Jean's sad. Poor, poor Ruby Jean."

Maybe it was jus a dream bout Morris an all, but I had to shake myself to stop all em voices in my head. I decided best thing was to get oudda bed an go out to the kitchen.

The house was quiet — yup, awful quiet. I thought bout how some toast an tea would make me feel better. But when I looked round there weren't no bread. I guess that's cause Nan dint take none oudda the freezer — on account of what happened to Pops. I decided to have frozen waffles instead.

Waitin for em waffles to pop up from the toaster I still hadda bad feelin from my dream. Started to think bout what Greg told Nan — somethin bout Mrs. Gentry makin arrangements for me to go somewhere. Then I membered how Millie dint think I should leave Woodlands an how Bernice said I might come back one day. Sides livin with Nan an Pops, I only had one other home — that was Woodlands. I got awful nervous thinkin bout it — yup, gotta urge to gouge my fingernails into my hands. But instead I jumped cause the waffles popped up suddenly from the toaster an scared me. I took em out an slathered em with lots of maple syrup. Couldn't help thinkin how I never got frozen waffles in Woodlands — nope, never. Don't know why, but those waffles dint taste so good — nope, not a'tall.

Sittin there in the kitchen, with the darkness lookin in the window at me, I started to get the shivers. Not cause of bein cold — nope, jus cause I was thinkin bout my dream an bout goin back to Woodlands. That's when I got a idea. It was a awful scary idea — yup, made me even more jittery than before.

Still shakin, I put the dirdy dishes in the sink an went back to my room. I took out the red backpack Pops bought me an started fillin it. I packed some clothes. I packed my favourite pictures too — the one with Gramma at Christmas, the one with the Ward 33 kids on

Canada Day, an the one with Nan an Pops at the park. I packed the clock Pops got me too. I dint knowed how to tell time — jus liked the sound it made. There was one more thing I packed in my red bag — Gramma's locket. I put it in the liddle pocket an zipped it up tight.

I thought bout lotsa things when I was gettin dressed. Like how I hoped Ronald wasn't gunna be mad at me for not comin back to Four Leaf to make flower boxes with him. He was gunna hafta teach somebody else how to do that job now. An I thought bout Mrs. Gentry too, an how she wasn't gunna be happy I went away without tellin her. "You must never leave the house without telling someone, Ruby Jean," she said long time ago. "This is a big city and you might get lost."

I looked out the window an was glad for the liddle bit of light comin from the street lamp. I sure was scared bout runnin away, but not so scared as havin to go back to Woodlands. I told myself, you gotta look after yourself now, Ruby Jean — yup, gotta run away fore it's too late. I said that cause I made myself a promise that day — yup, promised myself I weren't never goin back to Woodlands. Nope, never goin there again.

I put on my yellow jacket an backpack an went out the front door real quiet — quiet as a mouse. It was hard to leave cause it was the only place I really wanted to be. Then I blowed a kiss to Nan, an one to Pops in heaven.

When I got to Blundell Road I membered what Pops told me bout buses. "We've got buses going anywhere in the city you want to go. One day I'll teach you how to use them. How'd you like that, Ruby Jean?" But I dint have Pops to teach me no more. So I was jus gunna have to teach myself bout buses.

Pops said I was good at learnin things by watchin — like the time I learned to put the light switch together after he showed me. That's why I decided maybe if I jus watched other people I could figure out how to ride on the bus. In a liddle while a bus came an stopped in front of a man an he got on. Then it drove away. I watched more people an they all did the same thing every time those buses stopped.

I was nervous bout gettin on a bus — yup, awful nervous. But I went over to the place where em buses stopped at. Some more people came an waited too — yup, we all waited for a long time.

"The 6:50 must be late," said the man in a brown suit. Jus when I was startin to think bout findin nother place to wait the bus finally came. I stepped back an watched the others get on. The man in the suit said to me, "Ladies first." But I dint budge — nope, I wasn't gettin on till last.

The bus driver said, "Morning," to the man as he put some money into a box an sat down on a seat. I got on the bus after him an was gunna sit down too, but the driver man said, "You've got to pay if you want a ride." I dint have money — nope, all my money was in the Capital Credit Union. Gave it to em cause Pops said if I did they'd save it for me — for when I had a rainy day. It wasn't rainin that day — but I sure wished it was so I could have some of that money. "Well, haven't got all day. Are you going to pay or get off?"

I dint have money so I started to get off the bus. But the man in the suit said, "Just a minute, I've got enough to pay her fare." He dropped some coins into the box an waved for me to get on. So that's jus what I did — I got back on the bus an sat cross from him.

"Well, aren't you going to thank the kind gentleman?" the bus driver asked.

He made me think of Morris. I wanted to thank the man, but somehow I jus couldn't make a peep — nope, not even a liddle peep.

"That's fine, Driver. There's no need for her to thank me. I'm happy to do it." Then he smiled at me again.

I tried my best but jus couldn't smile back. That's cause I was too scared an sad an was tryin hard to be the invisible Ruby Jean again.

After a liddle while the sky got brighter with sunshine. An then the streets got awful busy with cars an trucks an more buses too. Every time the bus stopped more people got off an on.

I stayed on that bus for a long time. I dint knowed where I was goin but I thought maybe when I saw the right place I'd get off. After a long time the driver left an a new one took his place — an after him nother one. My legs got awful tired an my tummy started makin noises too. The lady sittin side me dint like that an got up an moved away.

The bus moaned loud an rocked back an forth too. That made me feel sleepy like a baby in a craddle. I dint knowed how long it was fore I woke up, but when I did my pants was wet an had a bad smell too. Nother thing — it was dark outside an the stores was closed an the streets looked empty.

"Okay, we're at the end of the line for this bus!" the driver yelled from the front. "She's going in for the night. Time to get off!"

I looked round — there weren't nobody else on the bus cept me. Still, I hoped maybe if I got very small an sat low in the seat the driver wouldn't notice me.

"C'mon, the bus is going into the station. You can't stay on — gotta get off here."

The bus door whooshed open. I got up an felt the pee dribble down my pants. But the worst part was my wobbly legs — yup, they was jus like Nan's spaghetti an so wiggly I almost fell down. I held my bag close with one hand an the back of the seats with the other.

"Drinking too much, eh?" the driver said. "You better find yourself a spot to sleep it off."

I dint knowed why he said I'd been drinkin too much. Maybe on account of I'd wet myself.

Soon's I stepped off, the bus door snapped shut hind me an it drove away. There was nobody round cept me. I stood there for a long time on account of me not knowin where I should go or what I should do. Like Mrs. Gentry said, I wasn't used to makin decisions. I always had someone else tellin me what to do. "Walk over here, Ruby Jean. Sit over there, Ruby Jean. Eat this, Ruby Jean. Go to sleep now, Ruby Jean." Now I dint have nobody to tell me what to do, but wished I did.

I was glad for the light comin from all em buildins an street lights — otherwise it'd be awful dark in that place. There was stores, but they was closed up an dark inside. Over top of em was windows with bits of light peekin out hind curtains. I think maybe inside em rooms was TVs playin an kettles boilin for tea an people talkin. After a liddle while, I started noticin the other people round about — someone was under a blanket in a doorway. An two more was lookin inside a big meddal garbage box down a dark alley. Cross the street some guys was standin by a small fire burnin in a bin. They was smokin cigrettes an havin a hard time standin straight — jus like me when I got off the bus.

Down the way I heard cars honkin an police sirens an voices coming from dark places. An there was so many words everywhere — cept I couldn't read em on account of me not bein so smart. I dint like the feelin bout that place an decided to find somewhere else. But jus when I stepped off the sidewalk a car came screechin up an made a awful honkin noise at me. Scared me awful so I jumped back on the sidewalk. That's when the man in the yellow car yelled at me. "Hey, you idiot, watch where you're going!"

Idiot. Imbecile. Retard. Those was things I been called lotsa times. Gramma said they was jus words an couldn't break my bones, but all the same it hurt every time somebody said em to me.

After I walked round for a long time I got tired — yup, awful tired. That's why I sure was glad when I found a liddle park with a bench to sit on.

"Got a cigarette?" said a growly voice from the shadows hind me jus after I sat down. I dint have cigrettes an the voice scared me. "Hey, you — I said, got a cigarette? I'll pay you a quarter."

The man stepped out from hind the tree. Even from far away I could see he was a dirty man. He came closer an jus looked at me for a long time. Then he walked away mumblin to hissclf.

I dint knowed that man a'tall, but I'd been round his kind my whole life. Yup, the kind of people whose eyes was like empty holes an shoulders bent so low they looked like they was carryin a awful heavy load. It was nothin but a whole lot of sadnesss that made em look like that.

Even though I was jittery scared in that place, I was too tired to walk anymore. I put on some clean pants from my bag an then put my pack on the bench like a pillow. Layed my head down on it an could hear the clock inside goin *tic tic tic* — helped me pretend I was at home in my bed.

Soon's I closed my eyes I heard Shirley in my head. She said, "Poor, poor Ruby Jean. She's sad cause Pops went away. No more Pops, no more Nan, an no more waffles. Poor, poor Ruby Jean." I tried makin her stop, but she jus kept talkin inside me. That made me feel lonesome — an more scared, an awful cold.

Nothin I could do bout feelin scared an lonesome. But I could do somethin bout bein cold. I sat up again an put on all my spare clothes — yup, put em all on till I bulged like a pillow. Dint knowed how I could still be shiverin — but I was. Yup, I jus shivered till every part of me hurt bad.

After a while I layed down again an started wonderin. Yup, I wondered if sleepin in the cold an bein hungry an lonely was really better than bein sent back to Woodlands. I dint have the answer an soon I got too tired of thinkin so much. I musta slept for a long time cause the nex thing I knowed the sky was gettin light again.

I sat up on the bench an watched a lady go by with a cup of somethin steamin hot an munchin on somethin.

She pointed down the road. "Soup kitchen's open. Better hurry — they've got eggs and muffins today."

Priddy soon other people was walkin toward that place she told me bout. I decided to follow em an see if I could get me some of em eggs an muffins too.

When I got up I suddenly membered my bag. I looked round for it but I dint see it nowhere. I dunno how, but it was gone — yup, wasn't on the bench, wasn't under the bench, wasn't no where round. I dint knowed how I lost it while I was sleepin, but I sure was awful sad bout it. Yup, no more pictures. No more *tic tic tic* from my clock or my priddy gold necklace from Gramma. I dint have nothin — nope, nothin cept the clothes I was wearin.

I might've stayed there feelin sad, only I was thinkin more bout bein hungry. I left the park an my bench an followed the tired an dirty people. Followed em to a stone buildin with a big Jesus cross on top an a long line of people waitin outside a liddle door.

"Gotta get in line if ya want to eat," a man said to me. "Or were you expecting the waiter to bring it to you?"

A bunch of em people laughed when the man said that. But I jus stayed there an watched. Yup, watched em people go through the door an then come out holdin a hot drink an somethin to eat.

When the line started gettin shorter, I said to myself, "You bedder get in there, Ruby Jean." When I went through the liddle door I saw two ladies wearin black scarves an black dresses.

"So sorry, everyone, but we're all out of eggs and muffins for today," one of the ladies said. "Lots of hot coffee and tea, though."

Then nother lady asked me, "What would you like, dear?"

I liked bein called dear, but it made me think of Nan.

"How about coffee?" she asked. Nope, dint want that. "Tea?" I nodded. "Sugar?" I nodded again. "Milk?" I nodded one last time.

The tea came oudda a big machine. No warmin the teapot first — nope, jus straight into the cup. That not the right way to make tea a'tall.

"I'm giving you two cups, dear — you look like you need it." When I was leavin that lady tole me, "God bless you." She looked at me the way Gramma used to — that made my eyes get water in em an so's I had a hard time seein my way out.

That hot tea made me feel nearly happy an it warmed me inside too. After I finished I dint knowed what to do with myself so I jus started walkin. The streets was quiet — not so many cars an only the dirty poor people walkin bout. Then after a while the sun got high in the sky an there was more people an cars everywhere. Ladies wearin priddy clothes an high heals, an men with ties an briefcases started showin up everywhere.

Dint take long fore my feet were tired an sore again. I couldn't find nother bench to sit on an so's I jus sat down on the cold, hard ground, in front of a buildin. I put my paper cups in front of me cause I was keepin em — yup, so's I could get more tea later from that lady in the black scarf.

A man went by when I was sittin there. But instead of walkin passed me like all the rest, he bent over my cup and throwed somethin inside. Made a clink sound.

I looked in my cup an saw some money. I dint knowed why that man did that, but I took the money out an put em in my pocket. After a liddle while of watchin busy people goin this way an that, nother man walked passed an dropped money in my cup. Then a lady did it too. Priddy soon I had a lotta liddle money.

I membered a time when Pops used some coins to get a candy bar oudda a machine. Maybe I could do that too — cept I dint knowed where to find a candy bar machine. That's why I decided to walk round some more an see if I could find one.

At first the only people I saw was the ones in a hurry to go places. Wondered how come I dint see none of em dirty soup kitchen ones. But then after a liddle while I started noticin them too. Yup, they was there ... in narrow lanes between buildins or in dirty corners by garbage bins or sittin on benches at bus stops or in the parks. Funny how they was hard to see at first — guess I jus needed to look more careful to see em.

One of em was a lady with a big cart — yup, a cart jus like the one me an Pops used at Spencer's Grocery store. Only her cart wasn't full of food. But she had things in that cart — lotsa things. I followed after her when she went down a narrow street an watched her lookin under garbage can lids. When she found somethin she'd put it in her cart. I followed her for a long time that mornin.

"Whatcha want?" she yelled after a while. I couldn't tell her cause I dint talk no more. "I ain't got nothin for you — go away." I followed some more cause I thought she was awful interestin. "Well? If ya got something to say, speak up." Nope, I dint have nothin to say. "Look, don't bug me, kid. I had a rough night. If you've got somethin to trade, let's do business. Otherwise, take off." Nope, dint have nothin to trade, nothin a'tall.

When the lady pushed her cart toward a busy road I hadda idea she was somebody who knowed things an so I should jus follow her some more. Good thing too cause she was goin back to that soup kitchen. After she got in the line I did too.

"Ya didn't answer me back there," cart lady said. "Ya got something to trade?" She looked down at my cup full of coins. "Say, I could use some cash. Ya wanna buy somethin off me?" She pulled back the plastic that was coverin her cart. I looked inside — she had clothes, an string, a pair of shoes, a glass jar with brown stuff, a blanket, some books an a pink heart-shaped box.

I petted her green blanket. "Can't have that — it's my best one. But ya can have this other one instead." She pulled out a blue blanket with rips an a big dirt spot. "I want five bucks for it." I offered her my cup of money. "Doesn't look like enough — did ya count it?" She was a dirty lady an she growled at me like a angry dog.

When the line started movin I started thinkin bout the tea I was gunna get an if maybe they was given out some eggs an muffins again. "Okay, look, I'll let ya have it for what's in the cup." I dint answer. "So is it a deal or not?" I held out my cup of money an poured it into her hands. Then she gave me the blanket an turned away. We dint talk no more after that. I hugged my new blanket as the people in front went in the door an then came out with somethin to eat an drink. I was gettin so excited bout havin somethin to eat I felt a liddle dizzy.

When me an the cart lady got to the door she told me, "Stay here an watch my stuff — you owe me that much." I dint knowed what I owed her, but I did what she said. Other people pushed passed me while I waited an waited. Finally, the cart lady came out. In her hand she had a cup of tea an a sandwich. Jus then my stomach let out a big growl an I knowed it needed a sandwich too. "Okay, I got it from here," she said an pushed her cart away.

Finally, it was my turn to go inside, but jus as I did I heard somebody say, "Sorry, but that's it for sandwiches today."

When I walked up to the counter the same lady in black said, "I know — tea with milk and sugar. Right?" I nodded. "You make sure you come earlier next time so you can get something to eat." I drank that tea awful fast. But it dint help me feel any better — nope, not a'tall.

Jus outside the soup kitchen I nearly fell down on the sidewalk. So that's why I sat down by the door an with my blanket pulled over me I closed my eyes. I decided I was jus gunna wait there ... dint knowed for how long … but I was gunna be the first one to get somethin to eat nex time the door opened.

I musta gone to sleep, cause the nex thing I knowed I was waken up to the sound of jinglin keys. For a minute I thought it was Millie come to unlock the big door to my room. I imagined her sayin, "Get up, Ruby Jean. And if you give me any trouble, I'll call the Boys." Then I opened my eyes an was awful glad it wasn't Millie's keys jinglin a'tall — nope, it was the nice lady in black.

"Good to see you're early this time. That means you're going to get some supper." I liked how the lady smiled at me, but it made me member how much I was missin Nan an Pops. "I just need to get things set up, dear. Won't be long now."

Hind me there was some others gettin in line, even the lady with the cart came round the corner. When she saw me she pushed passed all the others an came up to me.

"Ah, there ya are. Thanks for holdin my place." Then she looked at the man standin hind me. "Well? Make room there, buster. Gotta get in line here with my friend. She was just savin my space while I was makin a trip to the little girl's room." She looked at me an winked. "That blanket's a good one, eh?" I dint talk to her. But I was glad I had a blanket, specially cause it was gettin cold again with the sun gone away.

Jus then I smelled somethin licious comin oudda the door. Soon as it opened a voice from inside said, "Okay, soups on — come on in." I walked up to the counter where the lady in black held out a cup an a warm bundle. "That's cream of tomato soup and beef in a bun. Enjoy it, dear." She smiled at me awful nice, then started talkin to the cart lady hind me. "Hello, Mabel. How did you get at the front of the line so quickly? You didn't bud in, did you?"

"Now, Sister Irene, I haven't done that for a long time. That's my friend there. She saved me a space. Isn't that right?"

I dint answer her. Jus took my food an went outside so's I could eat.

That night was cold — yup, awful cold. I wrapped myself in my new blanket an layed on the bench in the park. I liked it there best cause there was light shinin down on me. I felt a lot better too with the pain in my tummy gone away.

I guess bein so tired I musta gone to sleep quick. I sure had lotsa dreams that night, but the one I member most was me standin in the shower at Woodlands, shakin from the cold water they was sprayin on me. Funny thing bout that dream was wakin up an findin raindrops splashin cross my face an makin my blanket all wet.

"For crying out loud, girl! Don't ya have sense to come in out of the rain?" I looked round to see who was talkin so cross at me. "Over here." I turned an saw a hand wavin at me from under some stairs. "Well, get in here. I ain't gonna hurt you."

I pulled my blanket round me tight an walked over to see who it was talkin like they knowed me. I dint wanna be standin in the rain all night, but I sure dint knowed if bein under stairs with a stranger was a good idea neither. I tried seein who was under there, but it was too dark.

"It's okay. It's me, Mabel." Mabel? I dint knowed no Mabel. "I'm the one that gotcha that blanket. See?" Then Mabel showed her face in the lamplight. "C'mon, hurry up. You're making me get all wet."

I bent down an crawled in under the stairs. First thing I noticed was how quiet it was under them stairs — yup, couldn't hardly hear the rain no more. But the best part was how warm an dry it was under there.

"Pretty nice, eh? This is my special place — nobody's allowed here except me and those I invite. So long as you remember that under the stairs of Pioneer Laundry belongs to Mabel you can sleep here for tonight — got it?" Mabel's voice was growly. I nodded at her. "I'm figuring you ain't been on the street very long. Nobody that's been at this for a while is gonna sleep out on a park bench in the rain — unless, of course, they're an idiot." I got hot on my face but dint think she could see.

Mabel pushed somethin at me. It was soft an dry. "Here, get that wet blanket off. You can put my parka on for tonight."

Soon's I put her coat on I started to get warm — as warm as a slice of bread in a toaster. I rubbed my face in the fuzzy collar — it was soft as Gramma's cat, Thomas.

"You ain't much for talkin, are ya, kid?" I dint answer. "Just as well. I'm tired — going back to sleep. See ya in the morning."

After that I curled up in a ball like Thomas the cat — that's cause I had a new friend an a dry place to sleep.

chapter 9

After that night Mabel showed me lots bout lookin after myself. Like how ya gotta find lotsa places to sleep at night jus in case somebody else gets there first or the police make you move. She tole me I gotta find places to stash my stuff too — cept I dint have no stuff. An she helped me find a big cardboard box too.

"Boxes are real nice to have now that it's starting to get cold. You better find a place to hide it, though — bound to be somebody try and steal a good box like this."

So far I got two good places for sleepin — the toilet at Pigeon Park an hind the Bamboo Smoke Shop in Chinatown. But the place I like sleepin best is with Mabel under the stairs — when she lets me.

"The homeless own this city at night," Mabel told me. "It's the only time nobody bothers us. We can sleep on the sidewalk or under bridges during a storm or even on the steps of the opera house when it's minus weather. And I shouldn't forget to mention garbage dumpsters — they can make a good place too when it's cold. Only, don't let yourself stay too long, like Loose Change Charlie. He didn't wake up on time one morning and got dumped into a garbage truck — poor old guy got crushed to death. Even sadder was how nobody noticed he was missing till his broken old body came tumbling out at the city dump."

Nother thing Mabel showed me was how to get to the Hastings Street Drop-In on Cordova. "It's okay in a real pinch," she said. "But you don't wanna go unless you absolutely have to ... like when it's freezing cold. Some people think we homeless will take anything, but even we got our limits."

Mabel started coughin an it got so bad I thought maybe she was gunna stop breathin. After lot more gaggin she finally spat out a big glob on the sidewalk.

"Phew! Now that's better. So anyway ... what was I sayin? Oh, yeah — homeless shelters ... got too many rules, that's for sure. Besides that they're dangerous — just about every time I stay in one I get robbed or get lice or some kind of disease. Fact, I got this bad chest cold last time I stayed at the mission. That's nearly four months ago — can't seem to shake it." Then she started coughin some more.

I usually went for somethin to eat at the church soup kitchen. But sometimes me an Mabel sat on the sidewalk an begged for money. When we did that we got to eat at McClucks or got a hot dog from Ernie's On-the-Go. Mabel always kept the money we dint spend on dinner.

"Let's face it, kid, the only reason people give us so much is because I'm brilliant at looking pathetic. I've got just the right sad and hungry look that makes them feel bad. It's only fair I should get to keep what's left over — you know, for being so talented."

I dint understand all Mabel said bout bein brilliantly pathetic, an I dint care if she kept the money neither. That's cause she was good to me — yup, she showed me lotsa things an she was my friend. An whenever I got money of my own she let me buy things off her — like my cushion an my Panasonic radio.

"Best radio ever made," Mabel told me.

I liked bein able to rest in the park with all em other homeless people — my head on a nice soft pillow an listenin to country music. Sometimes I wondered if maybe Norval was listenin too.

Nother thing I bought off Mabel was a red backpack. It looked lot like the one Pops gave me — cept it was dirty an the zipper was broke. I could put my blanket an pillow an radio inside an carry it on my back.

Some days me an Mabel was late gettin to the soup kitchen. If that happened we'd go to the alcholics meetin at the church an get juice an cookies. They served hot drinks too while the preacher talked bout God.

One mornin I crawled out from hind the Bamboo Smoke Shop an was hungry — yup, hungry as could be. I told myself, better get over to the soup kitchen fore they run oudda food. It was a good thing I got there on time cause they was givin out hot sausage rolls an tea that mornin ... an boy oh boy, it was licious. Dint see Mabel round.

I came back for lunch after spendin time at the park — they was handin out cheese sandwiches an for a extra treat Sister Irene gave out chocolate cake. That was awful licious too. Funny thing, I still dint see Mabel.

I decided to walk round an look for her. Went down Hastings an saw Betsy an John outside the liquor store. Saw Dean too — he was playin guitar for the people out front of the library. An there was Harsh too — collectin money in his tin cup. I went through Gastown an passed Woodwards Store too. But still dint see Mabel — nope, dint see her no where.

It was gettin dark an my tummy told me it was supper time. So I went back to the church soup kitchen an got in line hind Mr. and Mrs. Fay. That night we had tomato soup an bakin biscuits. They was good biscuits, but not so good as Nan's. I slept in the toilet at Pigeon Park, but I was lonely thinkin bout Mabel.

Nex day I went lookin for her gain at some of her best sleepin places — like the Hastings Street parkin lot ... hind

Fung's Dim Sum restaurant … an the stairwell in the old furniture factory. But still dint find her.

I membered that Mabel told me once she was a nutso. "I can't explain why or how it happens. All I know is now and then I get depressed — and trust me, kid, when I get like that you don't wanna be around me. Heck, I don't even wanna be around me." She showed me some red marks on her arms. "See these? Got one for every time I've tried to check out of this place. The really crazy thing is that people keep saving my worthless life."

After Mabel showed me her messed-up arms I showed her my messed-up hands. I had jus as many red marks from scratchin myself year after year. Funny thing bout that … I dint do that so much anymore.

"I can see you weren't a happy camper either, eh? That why you don't talk?" I nodded. "Ever been an inmate at Riverview?" I dint knowed bout Riverview. But there was a river ran passed Woodlands — maybe it was the same one as Riverview.

"Well, it was … twelve years ago. They had me locked up with all the other poor wretches on permanent mental vacation. But the first chance I had to get out of that place … zoom … I was gone. And I've been living on the streets ever since just so they don't catch up to me and put me back there. I guess you could say that's the best part of having no fixed address — nobody can find ya if ya don't wanna be found."

Mabel told me when she got those dark feelins inside her head she jus hadda be by herself. I wondered if that's how come I dint see her round lately. Boy, I sure missed Mabel — not as much as Nan an Pops — but all the same, she was my friend. I tried real hard not to think bout her or Nan an Pops, cause it jus made me feel awful bad.

It rained that day an after supper too. I got a idea I should sleep in Mabel's best spot — under the stairs at Pioneer Laundry — jus so's nobody else come an move in there. When I got as far as the park I was surprised cause I could see Mabel's cart cross the street. It wasn't there earlier. At first I got so excited my hands an heart started flappin bout. But when I got closer I thought it sure was awful funny that her cart was turned over an all her things dumped out on the ground. Her best blanket was in the dirt, her heart-shaped box smashed flat, an everythin else thrown round. That wasn't like Mabel to let her stuff get messed up. Then I noticed something else — all thrown round were pictures. I bent over an picked em up. That's when I figured somethin peculiar was goin on. Those pictures was of me — yup, me an Gramma at Christmas, me with Nan an Pops at the park, an nother one of me an the Ward 33 kids on Canada Day. I wondered how come Mabel had those pictures. Jus then I heard some moanin from under the stairs. I looked inside to see who it was.

"Kid, is that you?"

Mabel was there, but she dint sound so good. I crawled in an sat side her. She had a big cut on her head an bruises on her face too.

"I was praying you'd find me. I've been robbed, kid." Mabel sniffled an moaned. "The thieving swine dumped my cart and took my money and other things too. I tried to stop them, but they hit me. I fell down and hurt my head." She closed her eyes an sniffled some more. She dint want me to see she was cryin. "I feel like I'm startin to black out again … I need help … please … you gotta get help." Then Mabel's hand flopped onto the ground an she stopped movin. I tapped her shoulder, but she dint say nothin — nope, nothin a'tall.

I got awful scared after that — that's cause Mabel looked jus like Gramma fore the amblance took her to heaven. I sat there stabbin at my hands, an priddy soon I was cryin too — yup, cryin like a liddle baby. Couldn't understand why all the people I cared bout kept leavin me — Gramma, Grace, Pops … and now Mabel too. An there was never nothin I could do bout it … nope, I guess on account of me not bein so smart.

"Retard," I told myself. "Why'd you ever get borned, anyway?" I dug my fingernails into myself as hard as I could cause I was mad an hated myself for not bein like other people.

Jus then Mabel whispered, "You gotta get help … please, go get help."

After that Mabel went all quiet gain an I sat there feelin awful sad — yup, cause I knowed there was nothin I could do to help my friend. For some reason I membered what Gramma used to say bout me bein a precious gift from God.

I said to myself, "Gramma, I was never really precious — nope, not a'tall. And I could never be a gift from God neither on account of me not bein so smart."

I waited to hear Morris and Millie in my head sayin, "That's right, she's nothing but a retard." But that dint happen. Instead it was Gramma's voice.

She told me, "Ruby Jean Sharp, it's time you stopped feeling sorry for yourself. It doesn't matter what others think of you or if they call you names or if they don't know how precious you are — you'll just have to know it all by yourself. And anyway, there are plenty of people who see your true worth — like Grace and Nan and Pops and Mrs. Gentry … and Mabel too. But right now she needs your help. You're the only one who can do it, Ruby Jean."

I sat up straight an wiped away all em tears. I tried real hard to think what I could do to help Mabel. It was hard cause Morris kept tryin to get back inside my head by callin me names. But I told him to shut up. And that's when I got a idea — yup, I knowed what I hadda do. I patted Mabel real gentle.

"Don't worry, Mabel. I'm comin back." I crawled out from under the stairs an ran fast as I could — I hadda get to the church an find Sister Irene.

When I got there the soup kitchen door was closed up tight an nobody was round — nope, nobody. I banged an banged an banged on the door for a long time, but nobody came. I said to myself, "Okay, Ruby Jean, now what ya gunna do?"

Then I got nother idea — yup, the idea was tellin me to run round to the front of the church an up the stairs to the big wooden doors. I never been inside that church at night an I was fraid. But I dint stop — nope, I pulled hard as I could on em heavy doors till they opened enough for me to squeeze through. When I got inside — boy oh boy — I dint like how dark it was in there.

At first I was frozen to the spot. I had a hard time breathin too — I guess on account of I was scared. But then I heard Gramma inside my head again. "Mabel needs your help and you're the only one who can do it." I knowed she was right, so even if my legs dint want to I made em move forward into that dark place.

At first I dint see nothin — nope, only blackness. But slowly it stopped bein so dark in there an I could see somethin shiny. It was comin from the priddy glass windows an the big Jesus hangin on the gold cross. I knowed it wasn't the real Jesus.

It took an awful lotta tryin, but I finally called out, "Sssister … sssister … Sister Irene?" At first my voice was so quiet even I could hardly hear myself. I tried again — louder. "Ssister Irene, Mmmabel needs you! Sister?

Help!" Suddenly, the church wasn't dark no more — that's cause somebody put on the lights.

"What's the matter, child? Why are you calling for Sister Irene?"

I turned round an saw a lady wearin the same black scarf an dress as Sister Irene. "Mmmabel ... it's Mmmabel. Shhhhe's sick ... nnneeds help ... Sssister Irene gotta come help her."

"Try to calm yourself, dear. It sounds like we need an ambulance. I'll call 911. Where is your friend?"

"*Nooooo!*" I yelled. "No amblance. Don't want Mabel to go to heaven in an amblance."

"Heaven? For goodness' sake, child, what are you talking about? The ambulance will take your friend to the hospital. But first you need to tell me where she is."

I dint knowed how to tell her where Mabel was an even if I could I still dint want no amblance. Then I could feel somebody puttin a arm round me. I looked up an sawed it was Sister Irene. I was so glad I jus hadda hug her.

"Come ... come with me. Mmmmabel's sick. I'll show you." I pulled her hand an she followed me. We ran down those big church stairs an cross the street. I was gettin tired of runnin an I think Sister Irene was too. But we dint stop — nope, not a'tall. Ran down the lane, cross the park, an finally got all the way to Mabel's stairs. Sister Irene was breathin awful hard, but she looked underneath to see if Mabel was okay.

"Oh, dear, what's happened to you, Mabel?" Mabel dint answer. "Mabel, can you hear me?" Nope, Mabel couldn't hear a'tall. But then she moaned. "It looks like she's been beaten and might have a concussion. We need to get an ambulance immediately."

"*Noooo*, Sister Irene. Don't let the amblance take Mabel to heaven." My heart started jumpin round inside me awful bad. "If we let the amblance take her to heaven, I won't have nobody. Please don't let the amblance take Mabel."

Sister Irene grabbed my hands real hard an looked me straight in the eyes — jus like Grace used to if she was tellin me somethin important. "I promise — when the ambulance comes it will take Mabel straight to the hospital where she can get help for her injuries. Mabel will not go to heaven if we get help now! Do you understand?"

I dint knowed how come, but I believed Sister Irene. She told me to stay with Mabel an hold her hand. An that's jus what I did. Sister ran back to the church an called 911. A liddle while later I heard the siren comin. I got awful jittery again, but dint let go of Mabel's hand — nope, not for a second.

An jus like Sister Irene said, that amblance dint take Mabel to heaven, after all. Nope, that's cause Sister Irene an me made sure it dint. We followed it all the way to the hospital in the sister's car. That's when a nother funny thing happened — the amblance went to St. Paul's Hospital. At first I dint knowed why that name stayed in my mind. But then I membered — it was my hospital, the same one I was born at. Gramma used to say, "You came into this world on February 19, 1957, at St. Paul's Hospital. And it was one of the happiest days of my life." Yup, she really used to say that — over an over.

"Mabel is being treated right now, dear," said Sister Irene after talkin to the doctor. "Besides having a concussion and cuts, she has a mild case of pneumonia. The doctor said it was fortunate you found her when you did. You're a hero!"

I dint knowed why she was callin me that. I weren't no hero. Heroes was strong an smart an braver than anybody else.

"The doctor said we can go in to say hello in a short while. Let's sit in the waiting room."

Sister Irene took my hand an we sat on some chairs. Even after we sat down she held on to me. I liked that — yup, I liked to feel her warm hand holdin mine. An even when she looked at all the scratches an blood all over em — she dint let go — jus rubbed em gentle.

"Now that I know you can talk, will you tell me your name?" asked Sister Irene. She looked at me with her awful nice brown eyes — yup, she had brown eyes jus like Gramma's.

"My name's Ruby Jean Sharp. Gramma named me Ruby cause she said I was a precious jewel an called me Jean cause she said it meant I was a gift from God. Cept I'm not really precious or a gift from God."

"If that's what your grandmother thought, then it must be true."

"That's cause Gramma loved me — yup, she loved me even after the doctor tole her I was a retard. He said I got a extra chromosome — dunno what that is — but if I dint have it Mom an Harold wouldn't have left me at Woodlands." I dint member sayin so many words all at one time — nope, not since I was liddle. Back then me an Gramma talked a lot — yup, like two liddle love birds.

Funny thing bout talkin to Sister Irene that night … once I got started I couldn't seem to stop. I tole her bout Mom leavin me at Woodlands when I was eight … bout Peter slappin me … an bein put in the bad kid room. I told her how I dint like the uniforms touchin me an how the Boys broke my pink hair band from Grace … an how Susan an Norval was my only friends at Woodlands, cept for Mrs. Gentry.

"Cause of Mrs. Gentry I went to live with Nan an Pops. I had my own room — it had pictures on the wall, an a soft bed all fluffy an white, an a radio I could listen to at night so's I could fall asleep. But then Pops went to heaven in an amblance an they was gunna send me back to Woodlands. I dint want to go back there — nope, not a'tall." Maybe after bein silent for so long I jus had a lot to say. Dint think Sister Irene minded. So I talked an talked till I dint have nothin else to tell her.

"Well, Ruby Jean, that's an amazing story. And Mabel was fortunate you were there for her tonight."

Jus then a nurse came over to where we was sittin.

"If you want to say hello, the patient can see you now — but only for a few minutes."

Sister Irene held my hand an we walked down the hall. When we came in the room I thought it was an angel in bed an not Mabel. She looked clean an white — yup, white bandage round her head, white gown an white sheets too. She looked beaudiful. When she sawed us she smiled a liddle.

"Don't know what would've happened to me if you hadn't come along, kid."

"That's okay, Mabel. Yer my friend." Mabel looked awful surprised when I said that.

"Well, for crying out loud — so the cat didn't get your tongue, after all. I'm sure glad you're my friend too. But I'm getting tired of calling you kid. Got a name?"

"My name's Ruby Jean Sharp."

"You don't say? Well, that sure is a nice name. I knew another Ruby once — nice old lady."

Jus then the nurse came in an reminded us we had to go soon. She said we could come back in the mornin.

"Hey, Nurse, where's all my things?" Mabel asked. "I got a lot of important stuff, you know."

"I'm sorry. But there wasn't anything besides the clothes you arrived in," the nurse said.

Mabel growled a liddle an looked awful mad bout that.

"Oh, but there was this pretty locket," the nurse said. "I didn't want it to get lost, so I put it in this drawer for safekeeping."

She opened the liddle drawer. Inside was a gold necklace that looked a awful lot like the one Gramma gave me. I picked it up an opened it. Funny thing bout that — there inside was the picture of me an Gramma. I held the picture up so Mabel could see, but she dint look so good. Sides bein splotchy red her eyes were fillin with tears.

"Mabel, how come you gotta necklace jus like the one Gramma gave me?"

Sister Irene took the locket an looked at the liddle picture inside. She closed it an put it back in my hand. "Mabel, it looks like there's something you need to tell Ruby Jean."

When she dint say nothin I took the pictures I found on the ground side Mabel's cart outta my pocket an showed em to Mabel an Sister Irene too. But Mabel still dint say nothing. She jus looked out the window instead.

Finally, she said, "When you live on the street you do things … things that aren't very nice. Before I got to know ya, Ruby Jean, I saw you sleepin on the bench in the park. I guess you were out so cold and tired you didn't even notice when I pulled that pack out from under your head." Sister Irene gave Mabel some tissue to wipe her eyes. "After we got to be friends I wanted to find a way to give it all back — honest." She looked at me with awful sad eyes — yup, they was more sad than I ever seen. "It just got harder and harder to do as time went by. But honest, I was gonna give it all back. I was only wearing the necklace so nothing happened to it — well, and because it was so pretty."

I looked at that liddle locket Gramma gave me when I was eight. I thought bout how she gave it to me cause she loved me — yup, loved me a awful lot. I reached out for Mabel's hand an put the necklace in it.

"Mabel, yer my friend. I want to give you this present."

Mabel tried to give it back to me. "I can't take it. I stole it and I should never have done that. You've been a good friend to me, Ruby Jean. I'm sorry for what I've done. Please take the necklace back."

"Nope. Gramma gave it to me cause she loved me. An now I'm givin it to you … cause I love you, Mabel."

Mabel cried something awful after that. When the nurse came back into the room again she got cross with us.

"Seriously, you two have to leave right now so the patient can get some rest. Can't you see how upset she is from her ordeal. You come back tomorrow. Now off you go."

When me an Sister Irene was back inside her car I suddenly felt awful tired. I hoped nobody'd moved into Mabel's place under the stairs. It was a cold an rainy night an it sure would be a nice place to sleep.

"Ruby Jean, I was wondering if you'd tell me something?"

"Yup, I'd do anythin for you, Sister Irene. You helped me an Mabel."

"Well, then can you tell me how you ended up living on the streets?"

That was a hard question Sister Irene asked me. But I did my best to tell her the answer. "It's not that I wanna be homeless, Sister Irene. I jus dint never wanna go back to Woodlands. Bad's it is to be cold an hungry an have no home — it's bedder than bein yelled at an called names, or bein bossed round all the time an hit — and it's specially bedder than bein touched in places where ya don't wanna be touched.

"I had a nice home when I lived with Gramma. But she went to heaven. Nex best place in the world to live was with Nan an Pops. But when Pops went to heaven I was fraid of goin back to Woodlands. So I made myself a promise. I told myself, 'Ruby Jean, you never goin back there — nope, no matter what.' So that's why I sleep on the streets, Sister Irene."

"Hmm, I see." Then Sister Irene put her hand on mine. "Well, for tonight — would you come and sleep at my home?"

Sometimes I can jus tell bout a person — if they're good or bad. And I could tell Sister Irene was a nice lady — yup, awful nice.

"Okay, I'll sleep at your place tonight, Sister Irene."
I was secretly glad I dint have to sleep outside cause it
was awful cold an wet.

I dint member ever sleepin so good as that night on Sister
Irene's sofa. Sides bein real tired, I think I jus felt safe
there. I slept all through the night but all mornin too.

"Good afternoon, Ruby Jean," Sister Irene said when
I woke up. "My goodness, but you were tired. You must
have needed a good, long sleep. Are you hungry?"

I was still tired an could've slept some more, but I
liked to eat. Yup, probly my favourite thing to do in the
whole world. "Sister Irene, do you have toast an tea?"

She laughed. "Yes, but I'd be happy to make you
something more interesting — like an omelette or
porridge."

"That's okay. I like toast an tea best." I dint have
toast an tea since I left Nan an Pops's place. Sister Irene
let me make my own breakfast in her liddle kitchen. An
it turned out to be the best breakfast I ever had in my
life — yup, the best.

"Ruby Jean, I hope you won't be upset with me …"

Sister Irene looked jittery — like the way I got
sometimes. But I dint think I never could get mad at
her — nope, never.

"I called Social Services this morning while you were sleeping. They put me in touch with Mrs. Gentry — your caseworker. She says your family's been very worried about you and have been looking for you."

"But, Sister Irene, I got no family, cept Mabel." I got a sudden sad feelin cause I loved Nan. But she an Mrs. Gentry was gunna have to take me back to Woodlands. An no matter what I was never gunna go back there — nope, never.

A liddle later somebody knocked on Sister Irene's door.

"Ruby Jean, would you get that, please?" Sister Irene asked.

I dint mind, cause I liked to be helpful. But when I opened that door I got a awful big surprise — yup, it was Nan. She rushed in an gave me a hug — the kinda hugs my Gramma used to give me when I was liddle an she'd wrap me up inside her arms. But then I could tell there was someone else huggin me too — an when I looked up I saw who it was.

"Pops?" I cried. "Yer here. I thought you went to heaven in the amblance." I dint think I been so surprised in my life — nope, wasn't sure if I was sposed to laugh or cry so I did both.

"Is that what you thought, Ruby Jean?" Nan asked. "Did you think Pops died?" I nodded cause suddenly I couldn't say nothin on account of the cryin. "Pops did get sick, honey — very sick. That's why the ambulance came and took him to the hospital."

"The hospital? Jus like Mabel?"

"Who's Mabel, dear?"

I was too busy huggin Nan an Pops, so Sister Irene told em all bout Mabel.

"It seems Ruby Jean misunderstood what happened to Mr. Williams. Then she overheard you and your son and thought she'd be sent back to Woodlands. That's the reason she ran away."

Sister Irene told em all bout how I got food from the soup kitchen an slept hind the Bamboo Smoke Shop in Chinatown or in the toilet at Pigeon Park or under the stairs of Pioneer Laundry — when Mabel let me.

"I had no idea you thought I'd send you back to Woodlands, Ruby Jean," Nan said. "I'd never do that … you're family now. And as you can see, dear, Pops is quite well. He didn't go to heaven in the ambulance."

Pops laughed. "That's for sure. I'm right here for you Ruby Jean … and I want you to come home."

So I went home that day with Nan an Pops an got to sleep in my own bed. Nother thing — I had toast an tea three times fore I went to sleep that night. Nan an Pops took me to see Mabel the nex day — she looked lot bedder too. She tried givin me back the present I gave her. But I told her she had to keep it to member me by.

She cried some more after that — I dint mean to make her cry. I told her I was sorry.

"It's all right, Ruby Jean," Nan said. "You made her very happy."

I told Mabel I wasn't gunna be homeless no more. I told her Mrs. Gentry could find her a good home too — like mine. But Mabel dint like that idea.

"Just so ya don't think I'm not grateful, let me explain something. I've been on the streets for a long time. I know it's not the best life, but it's mine. I'm like one of those pioneers who came out west and opened up new territory. I live off the land, take what I need, and don't owe nobody nothin. I come and go as I please and don't do anything I don't want to — that's because I'm my own boss."

I think I knowed zackly what Mabel meant.

"A long time ago, before I was sent to Riverview, I used to have a job sorting letters for the post office. Most letters fit into the slots just fine — that's because they were all the same size. But every so often one came along that was too long or too wide and had to be put in the oversize drawer. For a letter sorter that was a nuisance — created more work, more effort."

I thought bout how nice it was that Mabel used to have a job at the post office.

"What I'm trying to say is I figure you and me are kind of like those oversize letters. We didn't fit into any of the usual places — we weren't like the others — so some people thought we had to be put somewhere separate. With you it was Woodlands. With me it was Riverview. But we got lucky — we got away. And just like you, I ain't never going back. That's why I chose the streets … it's where I want to be. So don't worry about me, kid. I'm a survivor." Then Mabel smiled at me. "Doesn't mean I'd say no to a little money now and then."

I never sawed Mabel again after that. Sometimes I thought bout her an bout goin to the soup kitchen to see how she was doin. But then I membered what she said — bout bein fine an bout not worryin bout her. Nan helped me to mail her some money care of Sister Irene. Got a letter back one day an Pops read it to me.

Dear Ruby Jean,

It was very kind of you to send money for Mabel. She is very fortunate to have a friend like you.

We're getting ready for winter and passing out blankets and coats every day to the needy. The church is setting up beds in the basement too for those willing to come in out of the cold. I'm glad you're not one of them.

Now that you're safely back home, dear girl, it's time to focus on the future. In the Bible there's a passage — it's one of my favourites: "I will restore to you the years that the locusts have eaten." Joel 2:25. Just remember, Ruby Jean, that good things come to those who trust and wait.

Your friend,
Sister Irene

I dint understand that part bout the locusts. That's cause I never learnt bout those kinda things before. Nan esplained it to me.

"I think what Sister Irene is trying to say is you've had some very difficult times in your life, but from now on things are going to be better — much better." Then Nan hugged me tight.

chapter 10

All that happened long time ago — yup, long, long ago. But then somethin else happened jus last week ... somethin I dint ever think would happen. I went back to Woodlands — yup, jus for a visit. Nobody lives there no more on account of it closed in 1996.

At first I dint want to go, but Nan said it was important us ones who survived be there for the celebration. They was openin a special garden — called the Woodlands Memorial Garden. There was speeches an singin an people cryin too — yup, a awful lot of cryin. The part I liked best was the cake an seein some of em kids who use to live at Woodlands. Cept they wasn't kids no more — some even had grey hair an wrinkles too. Dint see nobody from Ward 33 — nope, it was jus me. Wished I coulda seen Susan, but I dint knowed what happened to her. I never spected to see Norval on account of he died — yup, died long time ago. I always wondered if he ever got his wish to see a real-life hockey game — somehow I dint think so.

In that memorial garden they had a big monument with some of em old headstones — the ones the worker men dug up long time ago from the cemetery. Nan helped me find Willy Bennett's headstone. Norval would've liked that. Jus when I was bout to get myself nother piece of that cake, Nan said I had to meet somebody.

"Ruby Jean, I want you to meet Don Turner," she said. "He's a reporter from the newspaper. He'd like to talk to you about Woodlands."

Mr. Turner smiled at me. "Hi, Ruby Jean. Nice to meet you."

Nan an me walked with Mr. Turner to the bench cross from the headstone monument. We sat watchin the people. Some were readin the signs, others walked long the pathway to that sculpture of barred windows too high for anybody to see outta. I liked watchin the kids best — they was laughin an chasin each other round. Some was eatin cake. I hoped I was gunna get some more of that cake later too.

"Ruby Jean, it's been sixteen years since you left Woodlands. Do you think you could tell me a bit about what it was like growing up here?"

That Mr. Turner had a liddle tape recorder — it was so small it fit inside his pocket. I looked down at his hands — he was holdin a notepad an pen. He had real nice hands — yup, skin was smooth an fingers long an straight. Not a'tall like my hands with their red bumpy scars from all em years of scratchin an wrenchin em. An he sure looked like a nice man. But all the same I dint think I wanted to tell him bout my old life. I mostly tried not memberin so much bout it. Nan said I shouldn't never forget — she said I gotta member for the ones who can't.

I looked round the garden some more. I knowed it was the same place, but it dint look the same as back then. For one thing all em prickle trees have fat trunks now that make em look like big-bottomed ladies. And at the end of the garden, the old oak tree looks like a green ghost from all the moss coverin its branches. Jus then a train whistle blowed down by the river — jus like it use to when I was a liddle kid.

Down the hill was em old buildins — they looked same as they always did. Well, not zackly the same — they was empty an some of the windows was broken an the paint was peelin too. I had a funny fellin bout em buildings. Nobody lived there no more, but I kinda wondered if maybe there was spirits still inside. Ya know, spirits of sad liddle kids who died long time ago ... kids like Jimmie T ... who got trapped inside forever an ever. Were they still lookin out those barred windows, hopin to see someone who cared bout em? I looked hard at all em windows an waved — jus in case.

I told Mr. Turner he could turn on his recorder. I dint wanna be eight again, dint wanna walk through all em locked doors in my head — down bare hallways or into the bad kid room or the cold showers — but I knowed I had to. Yup, had to say somethin for all those ones who dint never get a chance.

"My name's Ruby Jean Sharp an I growed up in Woodlands School," I began to tell him. "That wasn't a nice place for a liddle kid — nope, not a nice place a'tall. Sometimes the uniforms was happy with me an called me Sharp-as-a-Tack. Then some days they wasn't happy cause I'd scratch an bite an wet myself. When I was bad the uniforms shouted at me an called me names, like retard. I sure dint like bein called that. They called me that on account of they dint think I was too smart, but they was wrong. I know lots of things. An I sure am glad people don't use that word no more ... ya know, the word *retard*. That's cause it's not nice ... hurts people's feelins."

I told Mr. Turner all bout the bad things at Woodlands an the good things too — like my friends Susan an Norval ... bout Christmas Day, when we got to eat turkey an soft lumpy tatoes an watched movies with lots of singin an angels an happy families. An bout some of the uniforms an volunteers who tried to help us kids.

"But Woodlands is all hind me now, Mr. Turner. I got a good life now livin with Nan an Pops. I knowed not everybody likes people like me ... an sometimes I don't like them neither. But we all gotta right to be here ... to be happy.

"Best part is I got a job an earn my own money. I make birdhouses an flower boxes at Cranfield's Nursery. How do ya like that for apples? On payday me an Ronald — that's my boyfriend — we take the bus to town to see the movies every Saturday night and I treat. An nother thing — I'm the one who decides what I'm gunna wear every day an what I'm gunna watch on TV an when I'm gunna go to bed. Now with all that good stuff wouldn't you be happy too, Mr. Turner?"

He laughed an switched off his liddle tape recorder. "Yes, I guess I would, Ruby Jean."

Jus then a liddle blond curly head popped up from hind the bench. "Aunt Ruby Jean, look! My shoe's undone again." Issie is Nan an Pops' granddaughter — she jus turned four. "Will you show me how to do it up again?"

I lifted her onto my knee an squeezed her tight. Couldn't help rubbin her soft hair the way I used to do to Barbra. "Boy oh boy ... you sure growed a lot, Issie. Is that cause you been eatin too much?" She smiled at me with eyes as big an round as sunflowers. That made me feel warm inside an I jus had to kiss her. "Say hello to Mr. Turner, Isabella."

Issie shook her head an pointed at her shoe.

"Okay, give me your hands an I'll show you how to tie your shoes." Then I sang the liddle song Mrs. Gentry taught me long time ago. "Criss cross an under the bridge, got to pull it tight. Make a loop but keep a tail, that's how to do it right. Then you take the other string, wrap it round the loop. Pull it through the peepin hole, now ya've got the scoop."

Jus then I noticed there was an old crow on the lawn not far away. His head was bent to one side like he was awful interested in what me an Issie was doin — yup, awful interested.

"Look, Issie, that's old Mister Crow." She jumped off my lap and tried to catch him. But he was havin none of that. He jus flew away — yup, flew off into the bright blue sky — free as a bird.

author's note

When I was a kid, there was one word that grated on my nerves like fingernails on a chalkboard: *retard*. That's because my older sister, who was born with Down syndrome, was often stared at, made fun of, and called names like *retard* by others who didn't know any better. When I was thirteen, I looked up the word in a dictionary and found that one definition simply read: "slow or delayed learning." I didn't think that sounded so bad — after all, everyone has something they find difficult to learn or master — and that took the sting out of the word for me.

At the time of Jane's birth in 1954 the attending doctor told my parents there was a good chance she would be blind, would never learn to walk, and wouldn't likely live beyond the age of five. He also explained there was no support available to help care for her and that she would be a burden to the family. His recommendation was to have her placed in an institution for the "mentally retarded" — a term used back then. The doctor's limited knowledge and attitude were quite typical for those days.

I'm grateful my parents weren't influenced by the dark predictions for Jane's future and instead brought her home from the hospital. As she grew, she had perfect vision. And she not only learned to walk, but to run, skip, and jump, too.

Jane lived into her mid-thirties. By the time of her death, she had a job and a boyfriend and lived in her own apartment. She had a full life and was loved by many. What more could one ask for from their time here on earth?

When I was younger, I had a fierce desire to defend my sister against the ridicule of others. Then, as a young adult, I enrolled in a college training program for special needs children and others with learning disabilities. One of my first jobs was working at Woodlands School. My employment in that bleak institution in New Westminster, British Columbia, lasted six long months. While I was there, I realized what my sister's life might have been like if my parents had taken the doctor's advice. I'm certain she would never have reached her full potential had she been one of those fifteen hundred people who spent their lives hidden out of sight and locked behind doors.

I left Woodlands to work for the Community Living Society, an organization started by parents and caring staff who fought to get residents out of Woodlands School and into group homes in the community. The Community Living Society and other associations like it were instrumental in bringing an end to the institution-alization of disabled people in British Columbia and seeing to it that Woodlands closed forever.

The characters and events in this novel are fictitious. However, Woodlands School, as mentioned earlier, actually did exist. There were many similar government-run institutions throughout Canada and the United States, but like Woodlands, many of them have been closed. Unfortunately, there are still such places to be found both north and south of the border.

Woodlands began in 1878 as the Provincial Lunatic Asylum. Soon after it opened, a report was written with the following description of the facility: "The place is gloomy in the extreme, the corridors narrow and sombre, the windows high and unnecessarily barred.... The establishment exceedingly overcrowded.... The patients being herded together more like cattle than human beings" (*Commission of Enquiry Report of the Provincial Asylum for the Insane, 1878*). The name of the place was changed in 1950 to Woodlands School, though at best there were only twelve teachers for more than fifteen hundred "students."

The residents of Woodlands were labelled as "severely or profoundly retarded," or as "morons." Some weren't mentally disabled at all but had physical disabilities or behaviour problems that were only made worse by the isolation, monotonous environment, and lack of normal human interactions. While some came to Woodlands as older children or even adults, others were abandoned as babies and knew no other home. Many lived out their lives behind its walls, locked metal doors, and jail-like windows. Ironically, some could even look out from this castle-like fortress to the B.C. Penitentiary next door, a maximum-security prison for society's worst criminals.

Some of the residents had visits from relatives, but most had no contact with the outside community. Those residents who were able to built friendships with other residents, then cried each night when they had to be separated. More often than not, the ones who needed the most attention and love got the least.

Woodlands, like many such institutions, was self-sufficient. It was staffed by medical and dental professionals, therapists, cooks, teachers, ward staff, and child-care workers. As a result, there was little contact with outside services such as public health, victim support, or police. In essence, it was a self-contained "city" with citizens who had no say in the running of their day-to-day life.

After Woodlands closed in 1996, the provincial government asked Ombudsman Dulcie McCallum to investigate the many complaints of abuse directed at the institution. Her report, *The Need to Know: Administrative Review of Woodlands School*, brought to light many of the problems inherent in institutions of this kind. She recounted that most residents had little if any contact with family or friends outside the institution. They had no control over any aspect of their lives. Even those who were capable were considered medically and legally incompetent as "retardates" and therefore treated as if they were unable to speak for themselves or had any intellectual insight whatsoever. Some children were used for drug experiments and genetic research — some of which are known today to be quite painful. And it wasn't uncommon for unclaimed bodies to be regularly donated to the University of British Columbia for research.

McCallum stated that Woodlands "was a perfect place for perpetrators seeking an opportunity to physically and sexually abuse children and adults who were silent, unable to complain, not knowing how or to whom to report or who would, in many instances, not be believed. Severe punishment and threats were used to dissuade children from reporting abuse."

Her report also stated that the cruel behaviour modification techniques were rationalized by staff who felt residents "didn't understand or feel pain, and in any event, required a strict disciplinary approach in order to learn." Little consideration was given to the fact that "bad behaviour was a response to confinement, only spending time with people of similar disabilities, absence of effort to socialize or integrate residents into normal life, boring, bland, sterile environment." One former resident of Woodlands described the place as "a garbage can for society's garbage kids."

Throughout the years there were many reported cases of physical and sexual abuse that leaked out. But according to reports, they were always handled internally. In most cases the investigation into the reported abuses was stalled by an apparent "code of silence" among the staff. Stories surfaced that staff who did report abuses were punished by some of their peers, threatened, transferred, and in one case drugged and institutionalized. As a result of peer expectations, abuse was usually brought to light by people visiting the ward, such as student nurses or family members.

In 1977 the B.C. government ordered all headstones to be removed from the institution's cemetery. The reasons aren't completely clear why this action was taken. Some speculate it was to appease the directors of the new Queen's Park Hospital next door, who felt it was disturbing for patients to gaze out their windows at a cemetery. Between 1977 and 1980 some eighteen hundred headstones were removed and recycled for such purposes as lining walkways and making a barbecue for staff. Many headstones were simply discarded in the creek or sold off as building supplies. The cemetery itself was made into a park.

At its height the population of Woodlands reached an estimated fifteen hundred residents. In the past there were no support groups or organizations for parents whose children had mental, behavioural, or physical disabilities. Although some thought institutionalization was the kindest treatment for these children, the very existence of facilities such as Woodlands testified to the general opinion that these people should be kept locked away and isolated from society.

McCallum's report paints a bleak picture of this infamous institution. However, in fairness it should be added that there were some staff members who did their best to care for the residents in a respectful and nurturing manner. And there are a few parents who felt their sons or daughters benefited from being placed there.

After Woodlands closed, it remained empty for many years, though the buildings were occasionally used by the film industry. Eventually, the provincial government sold the land to developers who began to erase all evidence of the institution's existence. During a period of public debate over what was to happen to the few remaining buildings, a terrible fire broke out on July 10, 2008. In a few short hours the flames destroyed all but the facade of the centre block and tower, the oldest part of the institution. Two days after the fire, developers were given permission to demolish and remove the debris, but no in-depth investigation has so far been conducted.

Today the cemetery has become the Woodlands Memorial Garden and honours the more than three thousand deceased individuals who were buried at the former Woodlands cemetery. To date only about nine hundred grave markers have been recovered. Officials say no more graves will be removed or dismantled.

The valuable real estate overlooking the Fraser River and the mountains beyond continues to be moulded into modern townhouses and apartment towers. Only the black monoliths covered in headstones at the back of the property are left to remind us all that more than a century of undervalued people once lived and died there.

> For the needs of the needy shall not be
> ignored forever;
> the hopes of the poor shall not always be
> crushed. (Psalms 9:18)

For more information on the Internet, check out *www. bcacl.org/index.cfm?act=main&call=A75B1B75*. To read the report written by Dulcie McCallum, see *www.bcacl. org/documents/Woodlands_Abuse/The_Need_to_Know. pdf*. To view *Asylum: A Long Last Look at Woodlands* by photographer and artist Michael de Courcy, go to *www. michaeldecourcy.com/asylum*. A teacher's guide for *Free as a Bird* is available at *www.dundurn.com/teachers*.

more great fiction for young people from Dundurn

Ghost Ride
by Marina Cohen
978-1-55488-438-4
$12.99

Eager to fit in at his new school, fourteen-year-old Sam McLean joins the popular Cody and his sidekick, Javon, on their midnight ghost riding, where the driver and passenger climb onto the hood of their moving car and dance. But something goes wrong, and soon mysterious messages appear on Cody's blog and anonymous notes are slid into Sam's locker. As Sam struggles with his conscience, a haunting question remains: Who else knows the truth?

Girl on the Other Side
by Deborah Kerbel
978-1-55488-443-8
$12.99

Despite their differences, Tabby and Lora have something in common — they're both harbouring dark secrets and a lot of pain. Although they've never been friends, a series of strange events causes their lives to crash together in ways neither could have ever imagined. When the dust finally settles and all their secrets are forced out into the light, will the girls be saved ... or destroyed?

Watcher
by Valerie Sherrard
978-1-55488-431-5
$12.99

Sixteen-year-old Porter Delancy has his future figured out, but his nice, neat plans are shaken when a man he believes may be his father suddenly appears in his Toronto neighbourhood. As Porter looks for answers, it begins to seem that all he's ever going to find are more questions.

Available at your favourite bookseller.

Tell us your story! What did you think of this book?
Join the conversation at www.definingcanada.ca/
tell-your-story by telling us what you think.

also by Gina McMurchy-Barber

Reading the Bones
A Peggy Henderson Adventure
978-1-55002-732-7
$11.99

Twelve-year-old Peggy Henderson is forced to live in a quiet British Columbia town with her aunt and uncle. She grows increasingly unhappy until she discovers a human skull in her backyard! The town was built on top of a five-thousand-year-old Coast Salish fishing village. With help, Peggy comes to know the ancient storyteller buried in her yard in a way few others can — by reading the bones.